THE PRICE OF BREAD

The Price
of Bread

Crysse Morrison

HOBNOB PRESS

First published in the United Kingdom
by The Hobnob Press,
8 Lock Warehouse, Severn Road, Gloucester GL1 2GA
www.hobnobpress.co.uk

British Library Cataloguing in Publication Data
A catalogue record for this book is available from the British Library

ISBN 978-1-906978-85-3

Typeset in Adobe Garamond Pro 11/13 pt
Typesetting and origination by John Chandler

Front cover illustration by Mutartis Boswell

Disclaimer:

This is a work of fiction. Historical events are either factually real or inspired by real situations, but the characters and their interactions are entirely imaginary.

TIME SCALE WINTER 1970 – WINTER 1971

Acknowledgements

I am massively indebted to Mo Robinson for both contributions and constructive editing advice. Thanks, also, to my writing group and friends for supportive encouragement.

I

THE FLAT

'WHERE's the party tonight?' Melissa asked, unwinding multicoloured knitted scarves and pulling off her fleecy mitts as she as she strode into the living room of Lee and Bruno's flat.

'Guy's place,' said Lee, adding quickly so Melissa wouldn't feel hurt by being asked to babysit rather than to join them, 'I don't think you know him, small bloke, sort of dapper.'

Melissa made a face to indicate scepticism that a friend of Lee and Bruno was likely to be dapper. She pushed back the heap of newspapers and children's clothes, and settled herself on the mattress that supplied the principal sitting area of the room.

The flat was typical of many leased to students in Belfast at that time: mainly above shops or unused buildings, with florid peeling wallpaper, dark paint, and damaged furniture. Bruno had stowed the settee with a broken arm in the coal bunker as soon as they arrived, replacing it with the big mattress onto which Melissa had now lowered herself amid the paraphernalia of the day's activities.

This was their living room in every effective sense: dining room, playroom, and in the evenings, with the children's activities piled into the wooden cot in the corner where the baby napped by day, this was their hub: the only room with a source of warmth. In the kitchen below, only the kettle and the gas cooker rings were ever used, and the icy bedrooms were strictly for sleeping – and under as many blankets as possible. They had been lucky to get this place so near the university and so cheaply, but it was cheap for a reason: it was previously just a storage area above a tobacconists shop and when that was closed, the only entry was up the steep, narrow, iron steps which led from the back yard to a small parapet outside the kitchen on the first floor, and thence to the internal stairs for the second flight. Anyone wanting access after the shop was closed had to use this fire-escape style strategy – and also negotiate the improvised barrier Bruno devised to safeguard their little boy, who was quick and venturesome. For supervised trips and party nights this was shifted, but most of their visitors were used to it, and to the heavy knocking required for access if the door was locked. Usually it wasn't, and their visitors simply walked in. Lee was happy with that arrangement: it suited her yearning for conviviality, and at that time – near the end of student term in the winter of 1970 – rain and cold were still her main concern.

Lee made an apologetic gesture as she grabbed some of the clutter and disappeared from the room to reallocate it.

'Coffee?' invited Bruno, scooping mugs from the table, floor, and mantlepiece. Melissa said 'If you're making it.' Elaine, a mature student who taught part-time at the College of Art and was currently lying in front of the fireguard reading, raised her head in vague enthusiasm. Paul, bending covetously over Bruno's guitar, nodded without pausing in his quiet chording.

Lee re-entered past her husband saying 'Yes more for me too please,' and then to Melissa 'You want a sandwich? It's over from lunch but I don't want it to waste, with the price of bread now – a loaf of plain is up to one-and-tenpence, and the woman in the shop says it'll soon be two shillings.'

Bruno paused in the doorway to say 'Wait till you see what next February's decimalisation will do to prices. No-one's ready for that.'

Lee nodded agreement. 'I was behind two women at the bus-stop last week and one goes to the other, "What do you think about this new money that's coming?" – like it's some sort of new film or something – and the other one just said back right away, very decided-sounding, "It'll never catch on." And she wasn't joking.'

'That's the tragedy,' said Elaine, looking up, 'They really know nothing except what's going on in Belfast. Which is of course the centre of the known world.'

'It's the things they say, and they way they say them – they don't even mean to be funny. Last time I was at the doctor's, there was this woman there with her little boy and she was saying 'He's been sicky-bad all week, I think he's got the measles,' and I was horrified – I mean, I had the baby with me and measles is contagious, isn't it?' I thought so – lucky we seem to have got away with it this time, if she was right. But this woman next to me asked what she was treating him with, and she said 'Just biscuits and brown lemonade.' I couldn't keep a straight face!'

'That reminds me, I meant to tell you,' Elaine said, 'It was so funny! I was in the Post Office last week and an old bloke in front of me was complaining the biro he'd been given wasn't working. The clerk told him to put his weight on it, and he tried again and I saw him write '9 stone' on his form!'

A quick spate of anecdotes followed, with Bruno joining in as he returned with coffee. There was the tale of the sandwich-board pusher who abandoned his promotion in the road whenever he stopped for a pint and was eventually taken to court where he pleaded 'Guilty but insane.' Everyone had a memory about that classic street demand 'You Protestant or Catholic?' Melissa's reply that she was an atheist had been met with 'Aye, well, this God ye don't believe in, is he the Protestant or the Catholic one?' Bruno then recalled a neighbour who needed two milkmen because she was forced to use the Catholic one who came early for her morning tea, taking only a single pint from him so that the rest of the day's order could go to the Protestant who didn't come till after ten.

Lee felt guilty sometimes about such conversations, especially among their English friends, but then the Irish did it too, didn't they? Deriding their own weird ways was like a national sport. There was even that 'John Pepper' column in the *Belfast Telegraph*, collecting all the funny things people had heard that week – not really wit, just daft comments – though not the religious ones of course. Those were only for telling in safe company. It was only the silly stuff that made it into the papers. The 'Nor'n Irish' loved nothing better than ridiculing themselves, it seemed. Grim levity for worrying times. None of the newspapers were to be trusted with actually printing the news, it seemed: The *Belfast Telegraph* was bigotedly anti-Catholic, and over the water the English reports were simply accepting the Unionist line that it was all the fault of the IRA, so nobody outside Ulster knew what was going on. Yet here everyone had chosen their colours – and in this part of the city those colours were red-white-and-blue. Union jacks, scrawled on fences and painted along kerbs, and massive murals of 'King Billy' on Sandy Row, were increasingly affirming a dogged allegiance dating back to 1690. Lee was thankful her 'crowd' was so amorphous, and proud of their open-mindedness, but she worried that maybe their parody teetered into bigotry of a different kind.

To change the subject now, she said to Paul 'Are you and Cara going tonight?'

Paul shrugged, turning again to the guitar, then clarified briefly 'Cara's not keen.'

Lee's eyes met Elaine's as they both re-interpreted: Cara is in one of her moods which is why I am lingering here drinking coffee instead of returning home with the cigarettes I used as a pretext for my escape.

Melissa, myopic but avid, said 'Why isn't she keen?'

'Well, she's …not feeling too grand. She had a rough day with Samantha, actually.'

Now even Melissa nodded understandingly. Samantha was Cara and Paul's demanding two-year-old, and they were all familiar with the phenomenon of Cara after a tussle with Samantha. Lee's triple response was usually sympathy for Paul and Cara, gratitude it wasn't her, and guilty fear that her selfish relief might trigger punishment from an avenging Fate. Paul had certainly changed in the last year. When she and Bruno had first met him, he had a cheerful indifference to the problems they shared: lack of money and its consequences. Paul's flippant sense of humour was usually received with groans, but accepted as a way of coping in a grim situation – and in Northern Ireland, a 'mixed marriage' was pretty grim.

Yet, Lee reflected once again in the slight silence that followed their sympathetic murmurs, everyone she knew seemed to be set on wedlock. While young couples in England chose to shock their parents by cohabiting, marriage was the new defiance here. This seemed hopeful to Lee: a commitment to disrupting the rules that defined communities on each side of the divide – a challenge to the old order, a way of defiantly saying *These children of the future have a mixed heritage, either claim them or die without descendants.*

Bruno was lucky since, although he'd married out of his sect, an English partner was a 'wild card' being probably heathen and therefore not counting, but in Ulster's 'mixed marriages' she had noticed that the Protestant parents tended to disown their sons – it was usually the boys who strayed – while the Catholic families often found more physical ways to express disapproval. Paul and Cara never divulged details, but Lee suspected both had suffered, and had come to feel strong attachment to Cara as well as an awed admiration of her classic beauty. With her green eyes and thick black hair, Lee saw Cara as a kind of fierce Irish tribal leader from medieval days, Gráinne Mhaol the warrior queen perhaps, and she couldn't understand why her friend so often seemed immersed in a kind of simmering anger. She had been like that since she had the baby, actually. Lee had come to the conclusion that Cara, like herself unexpectedly catapulted into motherhood, without a job to supplement their married couples' grant, simply couldn't tolerate living in the obscurity of a backstreet terrace. But, like John Lennon said, 'Life is what happens when you're making plans,' Lee thought. She hoped she wasn't smug, of course, but it was hard not to slightly pity Cara for her dissatisfaction when she looked around the entourage that regularly inhabited her own domain.

As Bruno handed round the coffees, no-one said anything more on the subject of Cara or her possible non-arrival at the party, and Melissa turned her attention to the languid form of Elaine, whose hands were undulating towards the mug like a caffeine-detecting radar system.

'And are you going?' she asked, and Elaine nodded slowly. 'Yeah, well, I'm going for a drink with these guys and then I might go along for a while. See what the scene is.'

'It might not be your scene, actually,' Lee started earnestly, and Bruno interrupted to ask how she knew it wouldn't be Elaine's scene. The ensuing wrangle about her possible scenic enjoyment was ignored by the coffee-sipping subject of the debate, and interrupted by Melissa.

'What's wrong with this guy, Guy? You're going, aren't you?'

This slightly floored Lee, who liked to think of herself and Bruno as skilfully skating around the perimeter of a wide range of social circles, and was reluctant to admit that this precious ability might actually be generally achievable. Also it was difficult to explain Guy without sounding patronising. They had met soon after Bruno and Lee moved into their flat, and Lee's first impression of Guy was that he was gay, an assumption that seemed to have occurred to everyone except Guy. He was obsessed with a 1950s world of pick-ups, dollies, and dates that never had any expectation of a permanent relationship. Lee had been girl of the month once, soon after they met. Their connection wouldn't have registered on any meter for torrid passion as it was limited to Guy singling her out at parties and expounding his ardour with regretful references to her married status. Since that phase passed, they had remained friends distantly and when they met at parties Lee could act as confidante to his latest unlikely amour. Every few months,

Guy threw a party featuring 'dollies' he had acquired recently, possibly for this purpose. Guy owned some kind of fancy goods business, from which he derived more funds than most of the people Lee knew, so there were a few bottles of spirits on offer at these events – certainly enough to break down inhibitions and cause a couple of rows if not a major trauma before the night was out.

This was partly the reason Lee had second thoughts after suggesting to Elaine that she might join them. She was also now anxious to make it clear to Melissa that Elaine's arrival at the flat had been unexpected, so Melissa wouldn't wonder why Elaine couldn't babysit and then she herself could have joined the group going to the party. Since this was impossible to convey with both success and subtlety, Lee was now trying instead to make the party sound a sufficient non-event for Melissa not to mind her exclusion, and yet suggest sufficient desirability for Elaine not to feel her babysitting time was being wasted. Such concerns obsessed Lee. She floundered futilely in the verbal complexities of this triple inference until Melissa, perceptively, said 'Well, I couldn't possibly go tonight – I've got far too much work to do for my thesis.'

Melissa was writing a thesis on the ability of speech to accurately reflect intention. She had been inspired by Wittgenstein in her final year of a Masters degree, and now continued to linger in Belfast on various mature student grants and in a small box-room near the Falls Road. Her project sounded fascinating to Lee, but Melissa's progress was continuously hampered by the complexities of testing. Each variant of test she developed fell at the hurdle of establishing a control and Melissa now seemed to have become stuck in a conviction this was an insuperable flaw, since accepting any control would presuppose the verbal effectiveness which her thesis intended to investigate. However, tonight she seemed either resigned to the conundrum or hopeful of a breakthrough, as she patted her Greek tapestry bag bulging with notes and texts, and settled herself purposefully on the mattress.

Paul finished his coffee and got up. 'I'd better be heading on,' he said, and remained fidgeting in the doorway. Elaine uncoiled slowly from her usual position on the floor and gathered her stuff towards her. 'Yeah, reckon I'd better be going too. I have to make my tea. See you eight, then – oh, which pub?'

Desultory discussion settled on The Ploughman's Head, and their guests departed. Melissa dug into her tapestry bag and produced several paperbacks and her thick ring-bound folder of notes. Lee picked up a copy of *Grimm's Fairy Tales* and looked at her enquiringly.

'Very relevant,' Melissa assured her, with her usual beaming smile. 'Seriously. I went to a brilliant lecture about the role of creative mythology in self-communication.'

She waved a dog-eared paperback with a black and purple cover, entitled *The Masks of God*. 'This is boundary breaking stuff, you know, I'm trying to work it into my overall thesis somehow. About how we all connect to each other through our personal myths, which come from the deep past – the major myths of every society.'

'I can see that,' Lee agreed, instantly fascinated as always on the infrequent occasions Melissa's thesis stumbled into a small oasis of positivity, 'All those fairy stories I read to the boys – they're important ways for them to process their feelings as they get more aware of the world – meeting emotions like jealousy, and anger.'

Melissa was still rummaging in her bag and now retrieved an apple which she thrust at Lee saying 'Have a bite.' Lee did, saying as she handed it back, 'That's not an experiment, is it? You didn't poison it? There's so many spells and curses in fairytales and myths.'

'Will you get yourself changed before I curse you myself?' Bruno urged, and leaving Melissa explaining 'Not a spell, just a Golden Delicious,' Lee made her way upstairs to the bedroom she and Bruno shared.

Here, the floor covered with brown lino and the walls smothered by a huge montage Lee had compiled from what in those days were jovially called 'the colour comics from the Sunday trendies.' Though she regularly deplored their commercial content and disparaged their money-centric attitude, for Lee they represented a connection with the fashion style of England, and a reminder that beyond the drizzle of Belfast there were other people, more affluent but also maybe more imaginative, with whom she could claim a kind of kinship. Lee had cut and pasted so many images from the supplements they effectively wallpapered the entire room. Around some nostalgic 'early Beatles' pictures and iconic film posters of favourite classics, Lee had found spaces to scrawl some of her favourite quotations: *Don't all lies eventually lead to truth* demanded the long legs of a bikini blonde. *Truth is constantly being formed from the solidification of illusions* warned the mists behind a lagoon. And, heavily underlined beside the 'Easy Rider' bike, a quotation from Wittgenstein: *The limit of my language is the limit of my world.*

Lee believed in the ability of words to tell the truth, if you found the right ones, and she believed truth was important – imperative in fact. This seemed to her the nearest to any kind of religion attainable.

Into this tabernacle Bruno entered.

'Jesus, you not changed yet?'

Lee had finished her make-up and was sitting on the bed huddled in her dressing-gown fiddling thoughtfully with her toes.

'I was hoping you'd help me decide. What shall I put on?'

Bruno, who always knew exactly what he intended to put on, began the swift process of clothes replacement by pulling off a green sweater and pulling on a pale blue one.

'What about your maxi?' he suggested as his head emerged.

'I wore that last time.'

'Your midi, then.'

'Not for a party. I'd feel frumpy.'

Firm tactics were required now. Bruno pulled off his jeans and replaced them with navy elephant cords while saying decisively '_I_ would like you to wear -'

'Yes?' said Lee anxiously. The two swift steps from bedside to mirror to lift their communal comb gave Bruno the opportunity to scan the wardrobe through the open door. '-your black mini-dress, with orange tights and black heels and that macrame choker Melissa made for you.' Bruno swiped the comb through his long curls with the confidence of a man who has satisfactorily solved a potentially tricky issue, as Lee nodded and moved to fulfil his demand.

'Do you think –' she began, since she could never resist the opportunity to probe some emotional problem when she had Bruno's captive attention, which she would have until he had completed combing his hair, pulling his long moustache critically, and turning sideways to the mirror to scrutinise the profile thus achieved – 'that Melissa minds that Elaine's going tonight?'

'No. Why should she? She wants to get on with her thesis.'

'Yes, but I just wish Elaine hadn't been here when she came. She's a very jealous person, you know.'

'Jealous?' Bruno looked astounded. 'What's she got to be jealous about?'

Lee wasn't fully sure, but she knew what it was like to walk into a room and find another person disconcertingly central, and to become suddenly uncertain of your own role. She tried to explain. Bruno looked baffled.

'Role? She's the baby-sitter, she offered. What's disconcerting about that?'

Bruno's rationality was unanswerable, and with his self-scrutiny complete he abandoned the discussion with a brief injunction to his wife to move herself swiftly or it would be closing time, and descended the stairs again.

Lee wished she could share his indifference. To her, relationships were precious, and infinitely precarious. She guarded her relationships with all those she loved with a tenacity that bordered on panic, seeing them as constantly assailed by threats of misunderstandings and misinterpretations, fearing her own inadequacy to protect them from such assaults. Would Melissa now think she loved her less? Had Elaine felt discouraged from joining them? Did her friends all actually realise how heart-breakingly, how necessarily, she loved them all?

Lee fixed the choker, sighed at her reflection and descended the stairs to receive Melissa's appreciative comments and reiterate the familiar list of instructions to cover every envisagable need of her children in her absence. She followed Bruno down the precarious iron steps into the back yard and they hurried down the short, dangerously dark, alley, to join the busy main street and head for the warm safety of the pub.

2

GUY'S PARTY

THE PLOUGHMAN'S HEAD was unusual among the pubs of Belfast in that the rebuilding after a partial burn-out had opted for the modern look in a big way, with flashing neon lights around the inn sign. This novelty might have proved a great attraction had word not got around that the head in question represented King Billy, so it was avoided by Catholics and Protestants alike under the impression it would be a focus for trouble. In fact within the pub nothing could be more trouble-free. It was all plastic sweet-peas and mauve strip lighting and PVC cushions. Lee liked it because it was so absurdly inappropriate for the area, and she followed Bruno into the lounge in happy anticipation of a night of unregretted excess.

Elaine was there already, having met a colleague from the College of Art where she taught part-time and decided to bypass tea and hair-wash to bring him along instead. She was now drooped over the laminated table-top looking rather gloomy as her companion embarked on a detailed critique of the decor.

'What on earth made you pick this place, Bruno?' Ian Kingston demanded, sounding elated at having specific grounds for his habitual attitude of superiority, 'It's dreadful, it literally hurts me. Not even camp, just terrible.' He was reminded, at length, of a similar assault to his sensitivities while reviewing the Edinburgh Festival the previous year, and embarked on an anecdote that blended name-dropping with obscure references which severely challenged Lee's determination to see the inner child in everyone to find compassion. Bruno had no such compunction.

'So long, then' he said heartily when Ian's rigmarole concluded with an intention to leave them.

'Be good' said Ian kindly to Lee, who was the only one still making eye contact. Elaine had already laid her head on her outstretched arms on the table to indicate the length of her lethargy and barely stirred as he left.

Elaine gave the kind of luxurious groan enjoyed by people when their exhaustion has only a few drinks and a party to cope with.

'Feeling rough?' asked Bruno of the long pale hair on the table. The hair lifted and Elaine's pale, rather lovely, face emerged. She gave another groan, this one a gentle assenting one, and then shook her hair to indicate purposeful reinvigoration. Lee watched her silent composure with admiration. At this moment, the lounge door opened and Cara and Paul walked in.

Cara looked splendid. She wore a long dress in deep blue, skirt slit at the side nearly to the waist and buttoned with demure tiny fabric-covered buttons. She seated herself beside them at the octagonal table, parting the skirt enough to reveal high-heeled, black suede, boots laced to the knee. Surprise at their arrival had immediately been overtaken by admiration at Cara's appearance and Lee, deeply impressed, noticed that all the gear was new. Cara had apparently overcome her recent black mood of poverty-obsession. Paul looked pleased and proud. His hair, newly-washed, dropped over his forehead softly. Being very tall, Paul easily looked lanky but tonight he looked simply elegant. He completed disposal of their coats and joined his wife at the table.

'What are you all drinking, then? Shorts?'

'What's the sudden affluence about, then?' inquired Bruno, not forgetting to add 'Whiskey.'

'Just got fed up scrimping. Life's not worth living if you can't splash out occasionally.'

At this modest expression of the temporary triumph of

his philosophy over his wife's, he patted her blue-draped knee and Cara smiled round radiantly and ordered a vodka and peppermint. Elaine's exhaustion was swiftly revived and she agreed to make it a four for whiskey.

'New trousers,' Bruno commented to Paul, and Lee noticed for the first time that he was wearing grey flares with a broad belt. This must have been what had given her the impression of such improvement in his appearance. 'Hey, they're great,' said Elaine – 'really smooth. And I just love that dress, Cara, it's fantastic.' Elaine was still wearing jeans. 'I meant to change." she added ruefully.

'What into?' asked Lee.

'My other jeans.'

The drinks arrived. Cara was clearly in an elevated mood. She leaned forward to Lee and proposed her new idea: she and Lee should share their children for one day a week, giving them each a free day. It would be a chance to look round the shops, she said, now it's so stressful taking a a pushchair into town, what with the bomb scares and soldiers suddenly closing roads around you. Lee was attracted by the idea of increased intimacy with Cara, though unsure of her ability to survive a day of Samantha. But Cara seemed so genuinely friendly, and so enthusiastic in her plans to devise educational games, that she agreed. After all, they had been friends before – close friends. It was up to her to make more effort, Lee decided, and to give Cara more support.

Bruno ordered another round and Elaine insisted on paying. 'After all, I'm the only one with a job,' she reasoned. Elaine's part-time lecturing was while she waited for a promised part in a play that had run into staging difficulties, Bruno was on a mature student's grant, and Paul was temporarily redundant.

Elaine talked about her students – 'great kids!' she called them, Cara and Lee talked about their children, and Bruno and Paul argued about a chord sequence in an Incredible String Band song. Cara's presence and ebullient mood seems to electrify the whole atmosphere to Lee, who was pronounced 'well away' by her husband when ten o'clock came and time was called. and they all proceeded down the road to Guy's.

The front door of his flat was open in spite of the cold night and they pushed into an atmosphere of dimmed lights and Tom Jones singing, and clamorous greeting from Guy.

'Eh baby you look fantastic' he called to the females, poking the males genially in their stomachs. 'Come on in, you're late, you're late!'

Guy had somehow got hold of a bough of mistletoe to hang in the hallway so all guests had to pass below it on arrival for the traditional social ritual.

'Why do we kiss under the mistletoe? Lee asked as she took off her coat and threw it onto the pile on the stairs, 'It's a parasite, isn't it?'

'So'm I, baby, so am I,' Guy responded genially, then, 'It's a Druid thing – we Celts were all Druids, you know.'

Lee raised her eyebrows to indicate her disbelief, and joined the others in the large front room. Tom Jones on the deck was now singing *It's not Unusual,* and plates with cocktail sticks holding chunks of cheese and pineapple stood on the available shelf space.

It was that sort of party. Lee felt in just the right mood for that sort of party. She had pulled off her coat and dropped it on the others on the stairs, following Guy into the main room which contained a sprinkling of girls she didn't know, a man who looked about thirty in evening dress, and several of the couples who Lee considered part of her 'circle' of acquaintance. Tim and Siobhan greeted them over plastic cups of home-made beer, Tim patting his hip pocket to indicate that strong stuff was available if discreetly petitioned later in the night.

Lee was pleased to see Tim and Siobhan. Her relationship with both had been erratic, after a dramatic start just over a year previously when Tim, out of a job and trying to make his name as a writer, was looking for somewhere to live. He himself was a practising atheist from staunchly protestant parentage, whereas Siobhan was a convent-reared catholic though now, like most of their friends, non-practising. Reaction to their announced engagement from both sets of parents had, at the time, astounded Lee. The Protestant parents used tight-lipped disapproval and heavy reproach, but the Catholic parents chose streams of abuse and a beating-up for Siobhan, organised by her mother and carried out by her brothers. On the fatal night designated for this summary justice Tim had recovered consciousness, after being knocked out by his brother-in-law-to-be, to see his fiancée's head being bashed against a wall, and had passed out again. Siobhan, returning dizzily to awareness after her battering, had seen the prone body of her lover and fainted once more. At this point the brothers may have felt God's will had sufficiently been done, or perhaps were a little frightened: they revived their victims with liquor and remorseful words, and an abatement of anguish was reached. When Lee first heard this story, over a year ago, she had thought this must surely be an unparalleled example of Irish bigotry overriding family feeling, but since then she'd observed enough of life in Belfast to find it unexceptional.

Despite the truce, Tim had remained eager to remove his betrothed from the septic bosom of her family and, lacking other options, they had moved in with Lee and Bruno. With no parameters or planned priorities, the arrangement had not worked particularly comfortably and by mutual agreement the menage broke up after a few months.

'I thought we could be like a mini-commune' Lee had mourned to Bruno, but he pointed out phlegmatically that Siobhan, as a new bride, was entitled to prefer a home of their own. Accidental meetings proved easier than Lee expected, visits began to be arranged, and now they were steady friends again. Lee had found the whole episode a baffling example of the complexity of human relationship and drew no useful conclusions, secretly feeling that much could be attributed to a lack of sexual frisson between the two couples. It may cause tension living in the same flat as an unattainable bloke you fancy, she reflected, but it's bound to be more tiresome when there's no mutual attraction at all.

Bruno and Tim, with a shared love of performance, had remained friends and even started a drama group together to supplement what both considered the cultural desert of the city. Their choice of Harold Pinter's one-act play *The Dumb Waiter,* much in vogue with students, needed hand-guns and Bruno had enterprisingly rented a couple that were used as starting-pistols from the sports shop.

'Disabled, of course, but I still had to get a licence for them,' he was now recalling to a growing group of listeners, 'even though they were drilled and plugged. Actually that was no problem, I got them from Donegal Pass police station. Tim kept the guns in his duffle bag and this one night, it was after midnight and pissing down with rain when we got to Checkpoint Charlie -'

'The hall we'd hired was in the north of the city, so we had to cross the Peace Line,' Tim interrupted to explain,

'And this bastard squaddie' Bruno continued, 'stops us and makes us get out and "assume the position".'

A gathering group was by now listening to this reminiscence and the two narrators, by now in their element, froze in that pose, holding their hands out to the audience.

'I had to drop the duffle bag and it went down with a thunk' Tim recalled, picking up his drink again. 'but luckily the squaddies didn't hear that because they were busy throwing everything out of our car out into the road to get soaked.'

Bruno nodded. 'They body-searched us, then told us to fuck off. So we picked up the duffle bag and scarpered. Jesus, the tension that night was unbelievable – just waiting for the buggers to find the guns!'

'What would have happened if they had?' Lee worried this

was an idiotic question as soon as she'd asked it, but apparently not, for Tim whistled and pulled a face and Bruno said 'A night in the cells very least.'

'If they didn't shoot you on the spot,' was the comment from another listener, but Guy had the last word.

'Why din't you put on a fecking pantomime, like a civilised drama group?' said Guy. 'Honestly – you students!'

The conversation passed to other things, but Lee was still troubled. She did remember Bruno coming home late during the nights of the production, which she hadn't attended because of the baby's night feeds, but she wondered now why she hadn't known about this before. Bruno had probably wanted to protect her from anxiety while the show was running, but he could have told her afterwards.

Now, below the balloons and streamers, Bruno and Siobhan had begun dancing to *It's Not Unusual*, the Tom Jones chart hit and still a classic. The record changed and the man who looked about thirty in a evening dress approached Lee, and they danced through several tracks of 'Beatles Greatest Hits'. They were the only two couples dancing at this stage, which pleased the exhibitionist in Lee. She and Bruno kept making little gestures towards each other as they danced until the man of about thirty got fed up and took Lee out to the kitchen to get another home-brew. Lee, who had been sick more times than enough on Guy's home-brew, poked around the carrier bags under table until she found some cans of beer.

The man of about thirty – Lee had forgotten his name again – now started to tell her that he'd been informed it was possible to distinguish on first sight between a Catholic and a Protestant in Ireland, and Lee, surprised at his scepticism, realised that his accent was not Ulster but Scots, and so like herself a foreigner.

'It's cultural upbringing they mean when they talk about Protestants and Catholics in this town, not religious conviction,' she explained. 'Actual beliefs don't come into it at all. My husband was stopped on a dark night by a gang and they weren't able to see his face so the ringleader asked the usual question 'Are you Catholic or Protestant?' and he said, 'I'm an atheist' and the guy just said, 'Are you a Catholic atheist or a Protestant atheist?' It's not your scruples they care about, it's your tribe. And yes, you can tell, as soon as you meet people – even I can do it, and I've only lived here two years.'

'What am I then?' said the Scotsman.

'You're Scots' Lee explained, adept after two years at Irish logic.

Their theoretical speculation of the intrinsic culture-conflict theory was interrupted by a practical demonstration. In the other room, some particularly drunk and particularly Protestant hangers-on of another batch of recently-arrived guests had started a fight with Siobhan's brothers who, now that past differences had been duly settled, continued to be frequent extras at parties that included their sister. There was a brief fracas and a few screams, and Lee's conversant disappeared to aid the rest of the males in booting out the late arrivals. Thus were the parties of Belfast in the winter of 1970, as British soldiers in the streets readied themselves with rubber bullets for more riots.

'Who did they come with?' asked Lee, wandering out to collect another can of beer from the a hallway.

'Ah well, that's a long story,' said Josh Brady, just arrived with his steady girlfriend Rowena. 'Us, actually,' he curtailed, 'We met them in the pub and to cut a long story short, they came along.' Rowena, flustered and apologetic, laughed nervously looking around hopefully for a sympathetic recognition of a familiar situation. 'That's my beer' added Josh, eyeing the can in Lee's hand.

'I got it from under that table.'

'Yeah, I put it there. We were here earlier, and then we went out to the boozer. What's wrong with Guy's stuff? There's a vat of it in the kitchen.'

'It's vicious,' Lee said simply, and Josh nodded.

'Go ahead, you're ok,' he said, and popped the can for her. 'And give me a dance, baby, I haven't danced with you for a month at least.'

When Lee had first come to Ulster she and Josh had dated briefly, before she met his friend Bruno and instantly set herself in pursuit of a relationship that had somehow developed into a marriage. Josh had since gone to England to find work, but discovered it "too fucking English" and returned, gravitating to Belfast for work. Their social circles had inevitably merged, and Rowena now solicited Lee on points of style because 'Josh thinks such a lot of you'. Lee was flattered, and glad that their abruptly-concluded affair had not withered into resentment. It was so important, Lee felt, to retain friendships, so essential that love is never left abandoned and useless – that everything should be somehow gathered and preserved, so that old loves enhance the new. So, that night, she moved to dance with Josh in a warm altruistic glow as if by doing so they could soar on some magical balloon far away from the reality of human struggles.

Later some first-year students crashed the party. One of them – long hair, Zapata moustache, brilliantly coloured fringed waistcoat – singled Lee out for a hard-sell approach. Lee thought him rather beautiful and danced erotically and exhibitionistically for a while, which seemed to encourage him to embark on a stream of unsubtle innuendo. Lee wanted to go on dancing so she responded for a while with a bright smile until she became bored. His banter seemed increasingly to be hostile now, with a challenge that eventually became explicit.

'Why won't you come upstairs with me?' demanded the student again and Lee answered this time.

'Possibly because my husband is dancing next to us.'

He appeared genuinely surprised for a moment, but quickly readjusted.

'You're married! My god you don't look old enough – you just don't look like a married woman.' And then he whispered intensely, fiercely, moving close to her ear,

'Alright then, you're married, you tell me this. What's another slice off the loaf to you? Eh? What's another slice off the loaf?'

Lee did not know. She felt threatened and antagonised. The student's pursuit no longer felt exciting and flattering, more an enactment of revenge for some grievance felt against the whole of womankind. It seemed now a demand for an act of intrinsic degradation, in atonement for the despicableness of all females – as though his savage begrudging desire was all her fault. There was nothing remotely sexually arousing in the way he whispered, fierce and despising 'What's another slice off the loaf to you?' Go on, he blatantly urged, admit you're either a slut or a hypocrite.

Lee was getting uneasy. Siobhan, noticing, came over with a thimbleful of whisky in a plastic cup.

'Here, I saved the last it for you. Wasn't it awful, that barney earlier? I nearly died with embarrassment, I was never so glad as when the boys left.'

Lee, looking round with some surprise, realised that Siobhan's brothers were not the only departures. Cara and Paul had also disappeared.

'What time is it?'

'Just after one. Who's sitting?'

'Melissa. We'd better get back, though, she likes to get up early when she's working. The thesis, you know.'

Lee left the student to Siobhan's expert handling and went in search of Bruno, who by this time was out in the kitchen helping Josh dispose of the legitimate brew. He agreed reluctantly to leave the job unfinished, and they got their coats.

'You're not going already, baby?' said Guy. 'The night is young – look, here's more people arriving.' A car had stopped outside the flat.

'We must go, Guy. Thanks ever so much, it was a lovely party. We're going to have one soon – a Christmas party. It's nearly Christmas.'

'Don't have one then,' said Rowena, 'We'll be away – everyone will be away doing their duty visit. Why don't you have one at the new year?'

'OK, then, New Year,' said Bruno, and called through the door 'Hey folks, everyone our place, New Years Eve. Spread the word!'

They left to a muffled sound of enthusiasm from within.

It was even colder than Lee had expected outside. Two people were coming up the path, from the car, to join the party. Lee recognised James and Fionnula StJohn, who had married two weeks earlier. She and Bruno didn't know them well, they were friends of Paul's. Or perhaps Cara's, thought Lee, remembering that Cara was said to have had a long affair with James some years before, before Samantha's arrival had irretrievably patterned out her future. It suddenly occurred to her that James was the only person they knew with enough money to run a car. And he's got a steady job, too, she thought. I wonder if Cara ever thinks of that.

'Hello,' said James, 'Party no good?'

'We have to leave early for the sitter.'

'Oh come on now, you can stay a bit longer now we're here!' James joked.

'Come to ours on New Year's Eve, will you?' said Bruno, taking Lee's hand for departure.

'When are you having your wife-swapping party?' called Lee on impulse as they left. She intended a jocular reference to his recently married status.

'When are you free?' replied James, grabbing at Lee as she passed him. Bruno, never one to miss a trick, moved forward to Fionnula, who squealed as he closed in on her. Both couples kissed enthusiastically and then parted cheerfully.

'Don't forget,' called Lee.

'I won't' responded James.

It was a fairly short walk home. Melissa, when approached, confessed herself tempted by another black coffee and Bruno was despatched to the kitchen. Lee changed quickly into her nightie and dressing gown and warmest jumper and squatted down by Melissa.

'How's it going?'

'Oh I don't want to talk about it at the moment actually.' This could mean anything from the germ of a new idea to total despair.

'Any sound from upstairs?'

'No – yes, little one cried once. I went and looked, but he was asleep. Good party?'

'Yes, well it was quite nice. I don't know if Elaine enjoyed it, I don't remember seeing her after we got there.'

'She left about twelve with that friend of Guy's in the evening dress suit,' volunteered Bruno, entering coffee-laden.

'Good God' said Lee, vaguely.

'Any dishy men there?' demanded Melissa, beaming to disguise her desire there should not have been.

'Only me,' said Bruno, beaming back. Melissa claimed to be choosey about her men. Melissa kicked him, spilling his coffee and then laughing throughout her unimpressive apology.

'Not really,' Lee answered, ignoring the wrangle over whether Melissa should get Bruno another cup or he should simply drink hers.

'What about your brigand?' asked Bruno, 'wasn't he dishy?'

'He looked alright,' conceded Lee. 'He was awfully… pushy, though. I don't like the pushy ones.'

Melissa said she couldn't bear the pushy ones, and began to collect her things together to leave.

'Thanks ever so much for sitting,' said Lee, and Melissa said it was ok and that she might be round on Sunday. 'I feel like a natter,' she said, 'we haven't had a natter for ages.'

Lee looked pleased, and as Bruno started to escort Melissa out she called 'Oh by the way, we're having a party at the New Year. Can you come?'

'Really? That'll be great – I'm not going home this

Christmas at all. In fact I'll probably be round here annoying you, but a party will be something special to look forward to. Well, see you Sunday.'

Bruno escorted her out onto the street and Lee curled up as close as she could get to the drooping wriggly red lines the electric fire, reflecting with satisfaction on the state of things. What a wide circle of friends we have, she thought complacently. How nice it is to know lots of people, and to be absolutely safe in an unshakeable relationship, like our marriage is. How lucky Bruno and I are. How lucky I am.

Her co-rhapsody appeared in the doorway, indicating the stairs with a tired thumb.

'Come on love, it's my turn to get up in the morning." he said.

3

THE WALL

WINTER SOLSTICE was approaching and the cold continued relentless. This was the week of the first scrawling, in orange chalk, on their back wall: GET OUT OR BE BURNED OUT, with a primitive criss-cross union jack, in case there was any doubt of origin.

Lee was aghast. 'Why?' she demanded – 'I mean, they must be able to see you're Protestant, Bruno – your family anyway, and I'm English!'

'Lee, we're sympathisers!'

It was the first time Lee had heard the term, but she realised with dull hopelessness what it must mean.

'So, tolerance is the enemy now?'

He shrugged assent. 'It's that age-old 'If you're not with us, you're agin us' thing.'

'Should we report it?'

Bruno was already scrubbing the lettering off the grey stones. 'Who to?' he said.

'Well, we've got a Police Station round the corner!'

'Let's just get it cleared, for now, Lee,' Bruno said. 'Maybe it's a one-off. Kids messing about, you know. It might not even be personal.'

Elaine dropped in that afternoon with some tee-shirts she was making for the children for a trying-on session. Lee, who made their clothes the way she'd made her dolls' outfits – by laying the child on the fabric on the floor and cutting around the outline – was delighted. Elaine had a sewing machine, so these were going to be splendid outfits. She brought up coffee from the kitchen and sat chatting with her friend as the children played.

'They're always so good!' Elaine commented approvingly.

Lee shrugged.

'Well, the baby can yell if he's hungry but they always seem to get engrossed in what they're doing. I think they probably feel comfortable whoever's here, whatever's happening, because we've aimed to create a kind of commune-feel for them.'

She gestured at the walls, where fluorescent purple wording, carefully painted on a poster created from a length of wrapping paper, displayed her personal mantra: the words of Kahlil Gibran, in his collection of teachings *The Prophet*, which Bruno had given her on their wedding day.

Your children are not your children, they are the sons and daughters of life's longing for itself. You may house their bodies but not their souls, for their souls dwell in the house of tomorrow, which you may not enter, not even in your dreams.

Elaine was familiar with the style of wall adornments that Lee favoured to transform the drab surroundings of their main living area – she had donated many of the Sunday magazine supplements Lee used to inspire the posters she created from the children's paints. Moving beyond cutting and pasting, Lee had developed a grid system to divide each chosen picture into sections which she mathematically reproduced, enlarged, on poster paper, infilling each section to a remarkably accurate degree. This system had been inspired by the Peter Sarstedt album cover as Lee was addicted to his song *The Sons of Cain*: reluctant to deface the actual cover, she had mathematically recreated the image, and her poster-sized version had since been joined by Beatles imagery inspired by Alan Aldridge. Elaine looked around her to see what else was new.

'You're such a flower child, Lee. Everyone else has grown out of 'Make Love Not War' and all that stuff – more's the pity. You still fly the flag.'

Lee gave an involuntary shudder at the word 'flag'. These

days it made her think of red, white, and blue chalk lines criss-crossing in primitive rectangles along the concrete walls.

'Well, I don't see it as a craze,' she explained in answer to the inference of Elaine's affectionate comment, 'I see it as a kind of essential energy – it's dormant, but so are seeds in the ground right now – and they regenerate. As long as these ideas exist, somewhere, there's a chance they could grow again… I have to believe that, or what kind of world have I brought my children into?'

'Not everywhere is as bad as this, Lee.'

'But it will be, if people give up on the values that matter. Peace and love, what was wrong with that?'

Elaine sighed. 'I dunno. I don't see any way out of it. I think I may go back to England if this stuff carries on. You know, my landlord asked me, when I moved in, what religion I was. I said 'I don't follow any religion.' He said, 'You need a religion if you're living in Ireland. Best choose Unionist.' I tried not to snigger, and I said, 'Unionism isn't a religion, it's a political movement!' He just stared at me. 'I'm not talking to you about politics!' he said, 'I'm just saying, when you take a religion, be Unionist!'

Elaine gave an ironic laugh that was more of a sigh, but Lee nodded unsurprised.

'I'd like to think we'll make a home here, though' she said. 'I know it's grim, but if people who dare to cross the divide all get pushed out, who's going to save the city?'

Elaine shrugged to suggest she wasn't as committed as Lee, and then nodded to show that she knew what Lee meant.

'The divide, yes, it's like an invisible Berlin wall. They can all tell on sight, can't they. Is it the eyes, do you think, or something else?'

'It's more instinctive than physical, I think,' Lee said, 'almost… visceral.' Something terrible became ingrained at a cellular level, she had often thought, when a vital strand within a community becomes demonised and impoverished by the dominant faction. Lee had wondered, when she first came to Ulster, how it was that her new friends all seemed to know, without a word spoken, what each others' places were in this poisonous construct – they didn't raise arms against each other, but they all knew their designated tribe.

'I can do it now,' she volunteered, 'Like, at Guy's party where there was the usual mix, mixed marriages you know, I was looking around and I just found I could tell. I dunno how.'

It had taken Lee a while before the insightful turning point arrived. Soon after they moved in, she and Bruno had been walking down a backstreet and a man had crossed the road to step alongside them saying, apparently genially, 'That's a nice green jacket your wee girl is wearing!' Bruno had not paused in his stride. 'Ah, she's English,' he said firmly, still looking ahead as he walked. The man mumbled something that sounded like an apology and moved away.

'What on earth was that about?' Lee asked, as soon as they were alone again.

'He just wanted to check whether he should duff me up or not.'

Lee digested this.

'So..' she suggested eventually, 'a prod would never wear green?'

'No-one would, round here. Asking for it.'

'But, because I was English, we were ok?'

Bruno nodded as though it were obvious. And it was, really, once Lee thought about it.. She didn't wear the jacket again.

And yet now, as she had told Elaine, Lee herself could tell. Small things had helped. Like, the day when she had such a bulk of shopping that she piled it all in the pushchair and steered it along with one hand, the other carrying the baby against her shoulder and with the little boy holding on to her coat, and a man had stopped her to say quietly, 'If you're in trouble we can give you a hand. Just give me your address and we can get your stuff to a safe place.' Lee was touched, not only by the offer, but that he had seen her as one of his tribe – not Irish, but a sympathiser. As Bruno had explained when the chalked warnings started appearing on their wall, sympathisers were the same as Catholics in this neighbourhood – in fact, they were betrayers, so they were worse.

Elaine, being English middle-class too, found Lee's decision to merge with her new tribe less baffling than Josh's girlfriend Rowena, who seemed to regard her as fascinating as an exotic lizard. Born and bred in Belfast, Rowena had quizzed her with mixed awe and total incomprehension.

'Did your mammy not mind you being here?' Rowena asked when they first came round to visit. 'Sure, the English papers are making it sound like it's trench warfare in the city.'

'Oh, I expect she's OK about it,' said Lee, never having considered the matter.

'Her mother's a bitch,' Bruno supplied helpfully, 'she'll be milking it.'

Lee thought about it, and nodded. It did sound plausible that her mother would be enjoying telling the neighbours how difficult it was for her.

'We're not big letter-writers,' she said, hoping that would cover the situation. But Rowena clearly wanted more, so Lee pointed out: 'There hadn't been the battles in the Falls when we first came here, so there wasn't anything about any troubles in Belfast in the English papers. They probably wouldn't even have known the Burntollet March set off from here – it was mostly Derry on the news.'

'I don't mean just the Troubles, Lee, it's you being over the water! You had a wee baby, and another on the way, did your family not miss you – your mammy, at least?'

Lee shrugged. 'I shouldn't think so. My mother never expected much of me, so I doubt she had many thoughts one way or the other. She never sent me any money to help out when we had to wait for Bruno's grant, and she's pretty well off, so that says how much she cares. I was trying to feed the four of us on two shillings a night, it was pretty grim.'

Rowena had put a sad face on so Lee added 'My father sent a posh hamper last Christmas which was kind of him. Not that anyone I know likes glazed tongue or quails' eggs but, you know, it was the thought...'

'Why do you talk about them like that, Lee? 'My mother, my father' – did you never say 'me Ma' or 'Mam'?'

'Well.. it was 'Mum' in England, for most people anyway. My mother didn't like that word though. She thought it was common. 'Common' was the worst thing, for her. Saying 'Mum' or 'Dad' was common. Playing in the street was common. Wearing plimsolls was common. Little wonder I never got picked for a game in the school playground, in my clonking lace-up shoes.'

'I think that's really sad,' Rowena had declared, and Lee realised that she was still talking about the miles that separated Lee's mother from her daughter and grandchildren. It was such moments of cross-purpose that reminded Lee she was living in another country with a very different culture – it was only similarities of language that made her think she understood anyone.

Elaine had left late in the afternoon, taking her part-made garments and leaving a bag of home-made biscuits, and Lee gathered up the coloured paper strips she had ready to make paper chains with the children next day. Something about these festive preparations reminded her of her own childhood at Primary School, and she recalled the conversation with Rowena, who had such a different view of family life. What, she wondered, did she want for her own children? Freedom, she thought. I want them to feel free.

She pulled out the photo album, never far from reach as the children loved looking at the snaps of themselves, and turned back to a photo from 1967, the 'summer of love' when she dropped out of sixth form and found a new way of life: outdoor pop concerts and free love. She hitch-hiked to Ireland, knowing next to nothing of the border, and had a whistle-stop education in Derry before meeting Bruno in Donegal. He came from a 'moderate' Protestant family, he told her, and had never joined an Orange march in his life – even though it was the best way to get hold of a trombone, which he longed to learn to play. Instead he had taught himself guitar from listening to *The Clancey Brothers* and she met him in a bar singing IRA songs.

'I thought you must be a Catholic!' she told him, confused, and he laughed.

'Ah sure the Micks have the best songs – we all sing 'em,'

He had no patience with the divisions either way, she was reassured to realise. Bruno and his friends were really quite like her, she thought: realistic, and open to new ways of looking at life. They had found a way to deal with the divisions: a gritty sense of humour about the long shadow of savage conflict that still lay visible across their lives. She realised their jocular sectarian prejudices were rooted in dark irony: 'Throw another Fenian on the fire,' when more heat was wanted, she learned, referenced the abuse of Catholics from the days of legendary Fionn mac Cumhail after the Scots protestants became their overlords. The lands had been reclaimed by rebellion but retained only until an Act of Settlement once again confiscated them. It was only when she discovered all this was way back in 1652 that Lee realised that, here in Ulster, the past wasn't so much 'lost in the mists of time' as embalmed: these memories were bloody but unbowed, blurred but still livid.

From Bruno and his friends she had learned about the 'Peoples' Democracy', a swiftly-doomed attempt to create common ground between the two sects through socialism and to bring common sense to the iniquitous voting system. This student-inspired initiative had died at Burntollet Bridge with the 'massacre' there the following year, but in 1968 when she and Bruno watched a march in Derry, it seemed a beacon of new hope. Lee had listened to the chant 'One Man – One Vote' with incredulity. 'What do they mean? We've had universal suffrage for fifty years!' she said, and Bruno answered 'Not over here.' He explained, with that terse, dry, resignation he and his friends all used when talking about Northern Ireland's politics, that only ratepayers were allowed the vote. Catholics, being poorer, were therefore often not home-owners and so had no right to participate in local elections. Often too their employers and landlords would acquire their votes to ensure Protestant domination in all polls, with the – largely Catholic – working population having no say in the matter.

Lee was politicised in an instant, and would have stayed furiously angry all day if she hadn't been distracted by a banner on behalf of Claude Wilton, a rare 'moderate' candidate, proclaiming *Vote for Claude, the Catholic Prod.* The crowd had taken this up as a chant, and their drawling of the vowel in his nickname gave the couplet a perfect rhyme scheme.

From this first political immersion, Lee realised she would remain an outsider – and she knew too that she would always stand with the misjudged and oppressed. All the Irish history she knew came from listening to their songs of protest. The hanging of brave Kevin Barry, the long ride of Kelly the boy from Killane, the fenian rally at the rising of the moon, the ambush of a doctor's car to bring guns to the rebels – she sang along to them all, and she knew which side she was on. The underdog. She knew what sidelining felt like and understood the casual cruelty of the strong. Lee had found a life purpose, and it was a Beatles song: *All you need is love.* Bruno postponed his college place, they had married, and set off to Greece, arriving about the same time as the military Junta, and lived for a summer in a hut on a Corfu beach.

Now Lee fingered the sun-bleached snaps of that idyllic time – images of herself in a multi-coloured long skirt dancing on the flat palm-roof of their hut as Bruno played Bob Dylan songs – *Hey Mister Tambourine Man* was her favourite. Her again, in that sweet little pink and purple mini-dress on a boat with someone from the hut camp who had taken them for a trip around the bay. They made money from Bruno's busking and bought food daily, throwing away what they hadn't eaten before the maggots could invade. It was intended to be a year's journey, travelling around the world – no plans, trusting the journey, but the first baby came so soon that his family, presuming this the reason for their hasty wedding, forgave them. And by the time Finbar was walking, he had a brother. They abandoned the hippy idyll dream and returned with Finn and baby Breff to Northern Ireland, where Bruno could complete his education enough to join the world of family-supporting fathers – not that the married man's grant was much help there. But Lee's priority was never to become like her mother, and in that respect she had no problem with her life-style at all.

It was ten o'clock next day, a lie-in morning for Lee, when Ariadne appeared in the doorway of the living-room after bumping her ramshackle pushchair up from the shop below. The pushchair held her daughter Titania who, though skinnier and smaller, was the same age as Finn. Ariadne was wearing pink-tinted sunglasses and a massive crimson woollen shawl and her usual expression of mingled anxiety and bravado. Desire to be loved gleamed from Ariadne's copper curls (self-dyed, tending to the vermillion), and the need to be cared-for pleaded from every cell, from her big crumpled bosom to her grubby ankle-length hemline. She looks like a gypsy granny trying to win at Crufts, thought Lee with exasperated affection.

'I've just popped round with these to see if they might fit one of your two,' explained Ariadne implausibly. She lived a good half-hour's walk away and never just popped anywhere. The items proffered were impossible: grime and fruit juice had smothered the pattern of the faded little sheet and the tiny knitted jacket was matted from countless bad washes. With downcast eyes, Lee mumbled her thanks.

'Actually, I was just going out,' she said, hating herself.

'Oh good,' beamed Ariadne, resilient as a punch-bag, 'I've got some shopping to do, I'll come with you." She chain-smoked menthol cigarettes and talked without pause as Lee, resigned to this compromise, moved about the room getting ready to go out.

Lee had met Ariadne at the Public Library some months previously and, ever avid to acquire new people for her eclectic collection of friends, brought her back for coffee. She had perhaps also been impressed by the fact that her bohemian-seeming new friend had a husband who was an artist, and might introduce them into yet another circle of acquaintances, all living arty lives and giving bohemian arty parties. As it transpired, Ariadne's husband, though he did little else, didn't really do any visible art, and Ariadne had no other friends or family – her mother, it seemed, had remarried an Italian count, and was constantly begging her to join them in Florence, or was it Venice? – but here in Belfast, LeRoy's creative genius, or something else unspecified, had been inspired so here they must stay… Ariadne's mother had warned her of this and begged her to leave him but her loyalty forbad it. He would die without her. And Lee, in short, was her only friend.

From that day on, Ariadne had clung to Lee like a drowning kitten. Lee would not have minded this, or Ariadne's fibs and absurd pretensions, except that Bruno, normally so tolerant, had put his put his foot down. That woman must not be in the flat while he was in it. And Cara and Paul found her ludicrous and didn't mind showing it, so Lee now always tried to get rid of Ariadne as soon as she appeared. Ariadne – perhaps somehow sensing this, perhaps out of innocent need – made this doubly difficult by always bringing gifts with her, usually obviously ill-afforded. Lee felt mean, and knew she should do, but it was horribly easy to collude with the witty mockery of Paul and Cara once Ariadne had gone, and that guilt provoked extra resentment when Ariadne's doleful eyes and hopeful hapless smile arrived, along with her paraphernalia of poverty and incompetence, bundling through their door.

Now, as they straddled the pavement with their pushchairs, Ariadne was spilling out her loneliness again.

'We've got a little kitten now! He's all grey and fluffy, he's ever so sweet. I have to buy him some tins of food – I don't think pussies eat chips!' Ariadne was always short of housekeeping money and she economised by buying potatoes, which were tuppence a pound, and making chips for almost every meal. As she was also always trying to lose weight – she needed to drop about four stone, Bruno reckoned – she dieted by having smaller helpings of chips. LeRoy appeared satisfied with this existence, as far as this strangely cadaverous and enigmatic character could be perceived to be satisfied with anything, and Ariadne supplemented her own diet with bars of slimmers' chocolate (frequently) and for her child, cheap sweets and lollipops (incessantly). Currently the child was busy spitting out smarties sucked from their tube.

'Titty!' cried Ariadne, and struck her a blow across her pallid little forehead, 'You naughty, naughty, little girl!' Titty began to wail thinly.

'Oh, don't, Ariadne,' begged Lee, though feeling the worst thing you can do at a time like this is interfere, 'She's probably had enough.'

She wished yet again that if Ariadne's cultural and romantic aspirations could not have been deflected from naming their child Titania, at least she could desist from shortening this to Titty. Cara and Paul were often ribald on the subject. Titania herself, it seemed to Lee, would have been more appropriately named Cobweb or Mustardseed. She was a pale little goblin with huge eyes who never tried to speak and flinched at sudden movements. Her tiny neck was marked with angry red patches and her little front teeth were quite rotten. Now for the thousandth time Lee wished she had the courage to turn to Ariadne and say, 'Throw away those rubbishy sweets you are destroying your daughter with, go and join Weight Watchers, go to the Samaritans, come out of your fantasy world and get the help I can't give you.' Instead, she stood silently as Ariadne stopped in front of the Open Door boutique and rhapsodised over a diaphanous champagne-coloured evening dress, saying 'When I've got my tummy down a little, that would be really me!'

'I think I'll send Titty's picture to London and get her a job as a child model' Ariadne continued chattily as they proceeded down towards Sandy Row. 'I used to do a little modelling, you know. That was how LeRoy met me. He always says one look and I swept him off his feet!' Lee had heard various versions of the first whirlwind encounter, including Paul's unkind suggestion they met as inmates of Purdysburn, the local psychiatric hospital. LeRoy didn't seem swept off his feet by his wife now, but then he didn't seem readily enlivened by anything. ('Perhaps he's going through a difficult patch with his art', Lee had said. 'Bollocks,' said Bruno.)

They reached Sandy Row, where you could get small eggs for one-and-tenpence a dozen and cheese for one-and-eight a pound though everyone said it would go up soon, when the new money came.

Lee bought some eggs and Ariadne bought a packet of chocolate biscuits which she broke open for both their children. When they came out of the shop it began to rain. Of course it would, Lee thought exasperatedly, when I've forgotten to bring the waterproof cover. They turned for home. There were two women in front of them at the traffic lights talking about the new Scandinavian restaurant that had opened uptown. 'I haven't been in,' said one, 'but they serve foreign food.' 'Oh?' said the other, incuriously, 'Chinese?'

God what a city, thought Lee, in a frenzy of frustration at the rain, Ariadne's chattering, and Belfast – incomparable, ignorant, Belfast. Where else would such insularity flourish and thrive like the weeds through the rain-soaked pavement cracks? Paucity of experience, paucity of interest, paucity of every human, curious, response. 'If it's not from here it may as well be Chinese, if they're not of our beliefs they may as well be our enemies.' It was all part of the same terrible, tragic, scenario – a cityscape of hot-house grown intolerance where habits of prejudice were ingrained as the grime on the civic buildings, painted as aggressively as the red-white-and-blue kerb stones along the Protestant side streets. On days like these it all made her shudder.

She left Ariadne in the street outside the shop by claiming the need to do some housework within, which while true felt mean, and steered Finn past the sweet counter where he was only allowed a penny liquorice, which she hoped would not ruin his teeth. The next step was to negotiate the children, one ahead and the other in her arms, up the unlit wooden stairs to their flat door, a flight more steps to pass the kitchen and finally to reach their living room, with its essential fire and the big metal guard where she draped their their wet coats before scurrying back down to collect the pushchair with its home-made child-seat and bump this up the stairs too. She was already beginning to feel anxious about the fact that after dark their only exit was the metal stairway from the back door in kitchen, unlit and with a difficult turn and narrow steps. It was difficult enough when the shop was closed on Sundays so she worried how she'd cope with the children if they ever needed a hurried escape at night. Since that chalked warning 'Get Out or be Burned Out' on their wall, she had a small case packed with passports, a clothing change, bottled feed and nappies, waiting by the window in case they had to make a quick getaway into the back alley and disappear into the dark side streets.

4

MELISSA'S VISITS

'I'M SORRY you're not well' said Melissa next Sunday evening, striding leather-booted into the general muddle of the living room at Lee and Bruno's. Lee was sitting pallidly on the floor by the fire, wearing a large sweater over a pair of Bruno's pyjamas – a fairly regular outfit for evenings when no social event was scheduled. Piles of fabric, mostly old wrap-around skirts and scraps of velvet and felt, lay about on the floor.

'O god I'm not ill, well, no more than I ever am.' said Lee, 'you know I'm never properly well these days.' It was true. A series of ailments kept Lee perpetually making apologetic trips to the doctor in futile hope of a potion to revitalise her and disperse the headaches and stomach pains that constantly assailed her. She was never the only one in the waiting room with such recurring problems, and rumours had started that these were the direct consequence of army bombardments in the Falls area each weekend, intended primarily to keep everyone indoors. The official line was that CS gas was harmless, but Gerry Fitt, leader of the newly founded SDLP party, was insisting that the gas caused severe ill-effects to health, especially to children and the old.

'It's the rain,' Lee explained as she cleared a space for Melissa in the colourful confusion, 'That stuff the soldiers use just hangs around in the atmosphere and every time it rains, it all comes back down and we get sick again.'

Melissa lowered herself into the space Lee had cleared and gestured around her. 'What's all this for?'

'I'm looking out some old clothes to make the boys waistcoats for Christmas.' Lee replied, 'I've got the pattern of their Clothkit ones and I'm making them velvet ones the same, with this braid on. By the way, could you sit again on Friday? We're going for a Chinese nosh-up with Paul and Cara.'

Melissa agreed, then added curiously 'I thought you weren't so keen on her these days?'

Lee put down a piece of purple corduroy she had been contemplating and tried to assemble her thoughts on the matter.

'It's a funny situation really. When we came here two years ago and first met them, we got really friendly, ever so quickly. I suppose it was something to do with us all being so hard up. We used to go to their place for a meal every Friday and they came to us every Saturday, and that was our social life, really. But we had a great time. We devised these incredibly cheap meals, like, just rice and boiled onions, with grated cheese stirred through, and we got in loads of cider – I can't usually stand the stuff, but I don't know, it seemed to be alright then. And then after Samantha was born, Cara seemed to get so angry about everything... I wanted to help her but she could be very... sort of scary, if you didn't agree with her. And the thing was, I almost never did –' Lee hesitated. She didn't want to say, 'she was getting so materialistic – she put no value on anything that wasn't costly,' because she didn't want to sound irritatingly virtuous, so she concluded '– on any subject that came up, we could be practically guaranteed to have different views.'

'I've never heard you argue with her,' Melissa said, making a sceptical face.

'We didn't actually argue – we just... didn't understand each other, so when she got moody, I pulled away. And now, somehow, we seem to be friends again. I couldn't have asked for anything better, I can't bear losing friendship. "Only connect" – you know – it really is the most important thing.'

Melissa nodded to show she recognised the reference to E M Forster's dictum. She produced a tortoiseshell comb from her bag and started to groom her thick dark hair while replying.

'You're far too vulnerable, Lee,' she pronounced. 'You set far too much importance on smooth relationships and you take failures too seriously. And you're obsessed with trying to make people like you! You shouldn't bother so much.'

Lee watched Melissa combing her hair with slow deliberation, looking to her like a wise gypsy as she squatted in her long red embroidered skirt beside the fire. A gypsy with psychic knowledge, thought Lee – she reads minds. Melissa had taught Lee her own personal doctrine: that everyone's default mode is to be defensive, and Lee found this liberating. It meant that her own anxiety was mirrored, or at least shared, by all those people she feared were judging her. Melissa's theory, couched in the abstruse vocabulary of a psychology research student, had merged helpfully with her own self-appraisal of hypersensitivity – the word she had learned for seeing life overly-vivid with colours of anguish. Melissa's theory was a practical antidote, and Melissa was a psychology student so she should know.

She picked up the corduroy again and laid it across a babygro to check if there would be enough fabric for a little jacket.

'Well, you know me, Melissa – relationships are the most important thing in my life. I truly believe the only thing that really matters is the way we connect to each other. It's more important than any abstract stuff, like morality, or politics – or anything. People who've made something good together, whether it's a marriage or a friendship, should never let it go bad – not just for themselves, but as a sort of moral duty to the whole world. We've got to keep extending outwards, connecting – because that's the only way everyone can ultimately be included. All the individual family units should be sort of ... cells, like in a beehive – starting with people committed to loving each other, but extending that community of love, until everybody's included.'

Melissa never had a problem with Lee's long monologues.

She put her comb away and hugged her knees thoughtfully, so Lee continued:

'Really, I'd like to live in a commune but I don't think I could overcome being bothered by petty things like waste of food, or the kinds of disagreements that happen in a large group. Last year I thought we could make our own, just a little one, here – that's what Tim and Siobhan living here was about for me, but it never really worked. Look, I haven't even given you a coffee – come down to the kitchen with me, and we can carry on talking. It's freezing though, better put your jacket back on.'

'Did you talk about what you expected of each other before they moved in?' Melissa wanted to know as they shivered down the steps to the draughty lower floor.

'Well, not in any detail.' Lee said, spooning out the instant powder into two mugs. 'I guess we thought things would just find the right flow, but those two hadn't had any chance to find out about living with each other, never mind with other people too. Basically, I don't think they "got" it. We all called it our mini-commune, but really it was just a shared flat to them – with all the restrictions of any shared accommodation. Tim's quite a private person,I suspect – and to Siobhan it probably just felt like being back in the nurses' hostel, only mixed. And I suppose my children didn't help – they had the bother of them and none of the rewards. With Paul and Cara, living close but not on top of each other, it will be completely different – intimate, but not interlocked. And with no expectations, so it can't go wrong, can it? I mean, it's not asking anything, just to be allowed to love. And we've been in and out of friendship with them, and somehow still hung on, so I'm sure we'll make it work this time.'

Melissa took her coffee mug and followed Lee back up to the living room. She sipped silently until Lee returned from checking on the children, and then asked

'Why is all this stuff so important to you, Lee? Keeping

close to everyone you've ever met – or the ones around you, anyway – why do you make such a big deal of it?'

Lee picked up the scissors to cut her corduroy, dolls-clothes style, into a basic shape that would fold over and, with trimming and sewing, a button and probably some appliqué, become the baby's christmas day outfit.

'Because it is a big deal, for me, Melissa. I don't believe in social rules, I just believe in people – and the only thing that absolutely everyone is capable of, even if they have no reasoning skills at all, is love. The solution the world needs has to be universal, so it has to be love, because that's the only thing every child in the world can do and understand. Once you realise that, and see how our world's got lost in crazy stuff like gods, and flags, then you want to just focus entirely on the loving – to kind of rectify the balance. I mean, we've still got the hippies and drop-outs, rejecting society's values completely, and that's great, but they're the extremists – and they want to stay that way – so it needs people like me and Bruno to alter things. We're inside the structure of society, basically accepting it, but not accepting current values.'

'They're the inevitable values of a capitalist society,' Melissa said, and Lee nodded vaguely, still on her own roll. and continued: 'I reject the claustrophobia of the conventional "family" unit: "my wife, my house, my job, my responsibilities," all accumulating in a pile of private ownership! I want to connect with as many different people as I can, and hopefully, in time, there'll be lots more people who feel like that, and we can redefine community. Forever!' Lee waved her arms wide to parody her ambition. Melissa laughed.

'And you came to Belfast! Talk about jumping in at the deep end. What was wrong with St Ives, or San Francisco!'

'Well, pragmatic reasons obviously – Bruno needs the qualification! And Ulster does need some people who aren't extremist, or everyone will kill each other.'

The sound of a police car's siren wailed past the window.

'D'you think Bernadette will be able to help, now she's gone to Westminster?' Lee asked, when she was audible again, 'I mean, it was the Catholic vote that got her into parliament, but she's a socialist, isn't she? Castro in a mini-skirt, they call her.'

Melissa nodded. 'Yeah. I've marched with Bernadette and you're right, she's not going to fight her voters' cause in London the way they want – but I honestly don't think she'll have any impact, anyway. For one thing England has never, ever, been interested in Ireland, and for another, the Palace of Westminster isn't the Students Union bar – they'll eat her alive and not even notice where they spit her bits.'

They finished their coffee in reflective silence.

'It's childhood segregation that maintains sectarianism,' Melissa said, and Lee nodded.

'But it's endemic now, like sewerage in ditchwater. People in this town, they simply can't envisage anything beyond their own experience, have you noticed?'

Melissa nodded, and Lee became suddenly conscious of the two of them as English women, outsiders, passing judgement with no real proximity to the beating heart – or hearts – of the city. She added quickly, 'I blame the newspapers and the telly, what they call the "news" is just the local stuff – you know, "Belfast Man Nearly Falls of Ladder", while over in Poland there's strikers and demonstrators getting shot by the army.'

'It's all on the international news, Lee.'

'But they don't watch that. They're brainwashed to think the only enemy is the people in the streets who don't share their religion. And they honestly believe the rest of the UK is segregated like they are – that all the new estates are designated Catholic or Protestant like here, with no sales allowed to the 'wrong' sect or the place would be torched. It's beyond ignorance, but it's not their fault, and it's really sad.'

'Well again, that's down to the education system here,' said Melissa, 'That's where it all starts. In the playground.'

Lee nodded, remembering Bruno telling her that as a child

he would watch the Catholic boys playing footie on the other side of the river, and wonder what it felt like to be them.

'How will you cope when the boys go to school?' Melissa asked now, 'Or will you home-school them? You could – with all the creative stuff and reading you do with them, but they might lose out with friends.'

Lee looked puzzled. School was two years off, at least – she hadn't even thought about it. Perhaps she had somehow assumed that the deadlock would break and the walls would come down and there would no longer be two 'sides' by then – or perhaps she had hoped they would live outside the conflict in a bubble of friendships in peaceful coexistence forever.

She was saved from replying as Melissa suddenly noticed the time and said hurriedly 'Can you put the tranny on for the 11 o'clock news? I heard there were two more blokes shot today.'

'Up the Falls?" Lee asked, twiddling the dials to tune into Radio One.

'I suppose so. It's dreadful the way the police do nothing to stop the UVF.'

'Oh they don't care – they're all on their side. Did I tell you, after we first moved I couldn't get into the flat one night because Bruno had fallen asleep and didn't hear me knocking – I was coming back from Elaine's and it was quite late – so I went to the cop shop to ask if one of them would help me get in. It's only round the corner, you'll have seen the sandbags they've piled up all around it now. This one cop was quite happy to come round and he started kicking the back door with his massive boot, and I was trying to tell him it opened outwards and he couldn't hear me for the racket, but luckily the noise woke Bruno before he'd mashed the door down. So we brought him in for a cup of tea and he stayed talking for ages, and the stuff he was saying was outrageous! I thought, why is he saying all this? He's got no way of knowing where my sympathies lie. Bruno was just sitting there grunting, saying 'oh aye' the way he does, but I kept wanting to argue. I shut up because Bruno was giving me the look, and then I realised the cop had simply assumed we were both anti-Catholic just because I was prepared to speak to him – even to ask for help when I was out alone on the street at night! Like, sectarianism trumps safety, or even survival!'

Melissa shrugged. 'No Catholic would go near a Police Station, whatever the situation. D'you blame them? I don't, after what I saw on the march to Derry, the way they laid into us at Burntollet bridge.'

Lee, deeming it too dangerous to take her baby and toddler without a more rugged pushchair, had not joined the Peoples' Democracy march but several of her friends had done so, and Melissa had been one of the faces shown on television on that notorious occasion, expostulating indignantly against the bland official denial of atrocities both condoned and committed by the police. It occurred to her now that maybe that brief exposure of Melissa's face on-screen had been recognised locally, and had triggered the threatening scrawls on their back wall. But a lot of their friends were students, so they would all probably be regarded as Civil Rights supporters, she thought, and then remembered she hadn't given Melissa the latest update.

'I meant to tell you, Bruno did go to the cop shop last time we got the warning on the wall. I reckon he thought showing his face in there was the best way to get the word out that we couldn't possibly be Fenians. I asked him how he got on and he said the cop on duty had suggested that maybe the flat "used to belong to some Catholics and it was meant for them." So he pointed out that wouldn't be much consolation when a petrol bomb came flying through our window. And you know what the cop said then? You'll laugh, because we did, but it's not funny. He said, "Don't worry, I'll get the B-men to keep an eye on you."' Lee thought she had a fair grasp of the alienation between the two factions in the city, but that response had shocked her. She knew the 'B specials', the team of armed civilians used ostensibly as 'border patrol', were notoriously virulently anti-Catholic – and she also knew that these acknowledged 'thugs in uniform' had officially been disbanded several months previously. Clearly nothing would change except in name, and not even that.

There was no mention of the dead men on the National News that night. After Melissa left, Lee turned the radio off and put on a record – a new favourite of hers: *Nothing Rhymed*, by an Irish singer-songwriter with the jokey name of Gilbert O'Sullivan. *Nothing good, nothing bad, nothing ventured, nothing gained, nothing still-born or lost*, she sang along, and reflected how effectively Faulkner and his Unionists had conjured up the IRA bogeyman to frighten the Protestant moderates away from the Peoples Rights movement. After Burntollet, moderates on both religious sides had dropped out from either anger or fear, and Bernadette, their homegrown St Joan, had probably now left Ireland forever. The world had looked on in mystification and then settled for misinformation. Brian Faulkner, vocally en route to his Prime Ministerial role, had insisted to the world that the IRA was puppet-master to this small socialist movement, and it seemed to Lee with hindsight that this, while derided at that time as absurdly untrue, had tragically been the trigger to all that followed: he had not only brought the Protestants sharply back in line, he had breathed life into a sleeping dragon too. Stories were circulating now of old IRA cells re-forming, of boys ardent for some desperate glory being approached to join up. Fathers and grandfathers were being asked if they still had contacts, and ancient connections were reviving. The Unionist party had created a monster for their own ends, but now that the buried bones of the Republic Army, alive still in song and story, had been dragged up and brandished, they were growing visceral flesh and beginning to stalk the land: the fantasy battle-flag that the Unionists had half-hoisted as warning had somehow become solid, in the real landscape.

Bruno was still out playing at a folk night, and Lee

was left brooding by the fire and shuddering at her own safe contentment. I am one of the lucky ones, she reflected, and the awareness seemed like a grim reproach. She listened out for the machine guns in Sandy Row half a mile away, cringing at the unfairness of existence. Life's rich tapestry, her mind phrased ironically – what a texture that is! Bloodstained, battered, exploded, napalmed, maimed, murdered, orphaned, widowed, crashed, crushed, starved, sick, losing, lost, deformed, imprisoned, suicidal – there seemed no limit to the words of hopelessness and agony appropriate to the human situation. And it's all so random! Here's me, with a loving man to look after me and my children, surrounded by caring friends – why me? And if me, why not everyone?

She looked out of the window beyond the sleet to the rooftops of the city, and thought how many people must be in tears right now. Children crying with cold, or pain, or fear – women crying because they can't feed their babies, or they've been hit, or they can't pay the rent – people homeless, wandering streets, hungry, fearful... and beyond the city, in the wild, animals trapped, hunted, with cubs left to starve... and beyond this land, across the ruthless sea, all over the world... an eternal reciprocity of anguish. Every failure is a failure of love, Lee reminded herself as she watched the raindrops on the window and wondered if Ruskin was wrong, and the elements did weep real tears.

Thus it was that Bruno found her on his return from the concert that night.

'I wish you wouldn't get so bloody morbid after these sessions with Melissa,' he said, 'She always seems to get you introspective, and leave you bubbling over with existential angst.'

He was holding two mugs of coffee. Lee took the one he extended towards her and shifted her stuff to make room for him.

'I didn't hear you knock! I must've been asleep.'

'I didn't, and yes, you were. I've locked up now.' Bruno said, and then, 'I'm gonna get a yale on that back door, Lee, so we have a key each. It's not safe just with the one for the two of us needing to go in and out when the shop's closed.'

'It's usually not locked anyway,' Lee pointed out.

Bruno sat down beside her. 'That's my point, Lee. I think we should keep the door locked, and each of us have a key. That way whether we're in or out, we're both ok. Just, keep it with you, not in the keyhole, and we both have access at all times.'

Lee digested this. Something else to mislay when it's not in its proper place, she thought worriedly.

'But what about our friends?

'What about them?'

'How will they get in?'

'Lee, they'll knock the door!'

I'll have to get up and let them in then, Lee thought, but she didn't say it because it would sound selfish. Perhaps it is, Lee thought, but she had so enjoyed those random unexpected arrivals that gave her a sense of her home as a hub, a place of community where all sorts of people gravitated and all were welcomed.

'Lee, it's for the children!' Her pause had been long enough for Bruno to feel he needed his fail-safe argument winner, and Lee agreed it was a good idea. That near-antique iron key had made their home a fortress, but only randomly: consistency was what they needed.

'And people can still walk in freely if they come up the stairs from the shop when it's open,' she pointed out brightly, cheering up at the thought.

Bruno sighed.

'Just, watch yourself love, that's all.'

5

MORE VISITS

NEXT MORNING brought Ariadne midway through breakfast, which was porridge as usual, with the milk warmed too since the air congealed it before it could be spooned up otherwise. Bruno concentrated exaggeratedly on feeding Breff his bowlful and Lee tried vainly to keep Finn interested in completing his, while Titty meandered about among his toys making little darts to clasp random items in her mottled, blue-with-cold hands. Her pale face, almost ivory-coloured today, was surrounded by the angora halo of a tiny, once sugar-pink, knitted baby-bonnet, stretched to fit her.

'I brought you these,' said Ariadne, rooting in her bag. Lee's heart sank. From deep within the scrabbled recesses, Ariadne produced two pairs of children's sunglasses. One was turquoise and one was yellow, and they had very dark, nearly black, plastic lenses.

'Aren't they cute?' demanded Ariadne, 'I saw them in Woollies, and I couldn't resist them. They were reduced, you know. Titty thought they were gorgeous, so I've got her two or three pairs. They can put them on and play at being film stars in St Tropez!'

Lee smiled weakly over the spoon of porridge she was waving at Finn as he strained backwards to see what Titty had just thrown across the floor. Bruno turned to view Ariadne with a look of unconcealed disgust and then turned silently away. Flushed with embarrassment and uncertainty, Lee said in an awkward rush of words, 'Ariadne that's awfully sweet of you and I'm terribly sorry I can't ask you to stop now, but I'm... in a bit of a hurry… I tell you what, I'm going to the library this afternoon – may I call at your place on the way back?' Her hastily invented request represented a total submission, and Ariadne seemed to recognise this as, after Lee had repeated both her apology and her suggestion, she collected her daughter and manoeuvred her pushchair towards the stairs. Lee sat feeling abashed as Ariadne's shrill remonstrations to her daughter echoed down both flights of stairs to the shop below.

'Thank god she's gone,' said Bruno, apparently oblivious to the coded drama associated with her departure, 'I'm not in till twelve today and I couldn't have stuck two hours of her.' Lee didn't point out there was no coincidence between his late lecture and Ariadne's dismissal but started clearing up the table and wondering where the library books were. She found *Green Eggs and Ham* quite easily – in the truck- and *Where The Wild Things Are* turned out to be under Finn's blankets. Paul came round shortly afterwards, and they joked about his narrow escape. 'Ariadne and her biggest boob, eh?' said Paul with a feigned shudder as he handed round the cigarettes.

In the afternoon Lee made her penitential trip to the library, calling afterwards as promised at Ariadne's basement flat off the Ormeau Road. In spite of the smell of wet nappies and stale milk she stayed as long as she could, in deference to the pathetic little feast of Munchmallows and crisps and squash prepared by Ariadne, leaving her with a reluctant promise to go Christmas shopping with her soon.

It was getting dark when she set off back home, and as they crossed the river Finn pointed down excitedly through the pillars of the bridge wall to the car lights reflected in the water. 'Look at the mirrors!' he was saying. Lee started conscientiously to explain but found herself lost for words, gazing equally rapt at the vivid reflections that flickered in the gloomy water. Even in a city of such dreariness, she thought, the river is irresistible. At least the river is beautiful.

Back at the flat she found Bruno and Paul listening to a

Rolling Stones album and engrossed in a discussion about the chords of *The Spider and the Fly.*

'Seems fairly simple – pretty standard progression,' Bruno was saying, while Paul was suggesting, 'If you get a walking bass going behind it? I'll just stick with full chords.'

'Sure, fire ahead. Yeah, that's sounding good…' Bruno waved at Lee: 'Hi love, is it me to do bedtime?'

It was, but they seemed so happily engrossed she said, 'You're alright. I'll do it – we got a book about cars from the library and I've promised to read with them.'

'Ah great… Sounding good, Paul.'

'OK if I have a bath, after they're settled?' Lee asked. '

'Sure. Oh, yeah, there we go. Watch out, Jagger!

They were arguing amicably about whether Leonard Cohen was a worse singer than Bob Dylan when she came down.

'Songs to slit your wrists by,' Paul was saying.

'You'll listen out for them?' she reminded Bruno, and he said 'Sure. The thing you don't realise is, Cohen's a poet. You have to *listen!*'

'I'll make sure he does,' Paul said reassuringly to her, then, 'His tunes are crap, too. A minor and G, and that's your lot.'

'Oh, you think? Go on then. Play *Suzanne* in A minor and G and see how far you get. Cheers love, see you in a bit.'

Lee collected her yoga book and set off to Ian's.

Ian's bathroom wasn't over-warm but it wasn't icy with fungoid stalactites, and all his towels were black so she could lay one down on the floor and lie on it to practice postures. During their hot and heady days in Greece, Lee had perfected – in her own eyes – several basic yoga poses, and had now acquired a slim book called 'Teach Yourself YOGA'. Disappointingly, there seemed to be very few exercises and the only illustrated pose was sitting down and breathing, which Lee felt she had pretty well mastered, but she decided to persevere with the text. Now warm from her bath and still naked, she was reading it in half-shoulder-stand, and had reached *Recommended Foods* which curiously included sugar, sugar candy, and ghee, and *Injurious Foods* which disappointingly included intoxicating liquors as well as onion and fish.

She flipped the pages and read *'When things are examined objectively, without heat or passion, one ceases to become attached to them.'*

And what's the point of that? Lee thought – there's no connection without attachment, so what we need is to communicate and accept each others' views. Then she started thinking how massively difficult both those things were and pushed the book away. Sill on her towel mat, she raised her legs steadily into full shoulder stand, then slowly back down to the floor with her pelvis still high, into a perfect bridge. Wow, she thought, holding the pose for a few moments before lowering her body backwards into a seated position just in time to see the bathroom door in front of her quietly closing. One good thing about Ian, Lee thought as she quickly dressed, is he'll pretend it never happened, so I can still come here for baths.

Ariadne arrived next morning with avid anticipation and a packet of pink balloons.

'I thought they'd look pretty on our pushchairs as we go into town,' she said, 'And I'm sure Bruno's got enough puff to blow them up for us!'

Bruno cleared his throat and gestured his chest to suggest an urgent throat condition, collected up his cereal bowl and removed himself to a safer, albeit colder, room.

'Oh, does it have to be today?' Lee had been looking forward to a rare morning with Bruno on their own. 'Could we go some other time?' Ariadne looked stricken, then beamed hopefully. 'You mean the Sales?'

Lee, who had successfully avoided any shop with 'Sale' posted on its window throughout her entire life, settled for the lesser evil of getting it over with now, and the two of them set off with their pushchairs towards the corner where Robinson and Cleaver stood grimy and splendid, its copper-clad turrets spy-holes to the grey, litter-strewn, streets six floors below, looking more like a foreign embassy than a place of trade.

'I'm not going to buy anything,' Ariadne confided, exasperatingly, when they eventually manoeuvred the army barriers to join the crowd of shoppers in the city centre, 'I just like to look and dream!'

At that moment there was a grating racket ahead which Lee could just about see through the throng was caused by soldiers dragging panels of what looked like caging across the pavement and road. Brakes screeched, and several voices called out 'Bomb Scare!' and then there were louder screams as boys in bright check scarves came running past at precipitous speed.

An extraordinary frisson ran through the crowd, not so much fear as excitement it seemed to Lee – almost exhilaration as if, in these tedious days of cold and dread, something was actually happening. And then the jostling began. Shouts of random expletives mingled with more specific appeals to the deity, and names of friends mislaid in the moving throng that had suddenly stalled into a crush.

Lee's immediate concern was for Finn, secured into his travel seat across the pushchair where the baby, luckily still sleeping, was protected by the hood she had already erected against the wind. Her pushchair had a long chassis, but the child-seat was home-made: it was sturdy enough for a toddler like Finn, who wasn't heavy and didn't wriggle, but it had never been tested in a panicking crowd. Lee usually unclipped Finn and carried him when faced with anything more complex than the kerb, and her instinct now was to do this and to hold him close, but she suddenly realised that the screeching sound she urgently wanted to get away from was issuing from Ariadne. For some reason inexplicable to Lee, Ariadne's immediate response had been to hurtle herself backwards as fast as she could, which was not fast at all and was causing the crowd behind her to get really angry as their feet were trampled and their children blundered into. Ariadne seemed unaware of this as her eyes were tight shut and she continued to scream.

Lee, on auto pilot, grabbed the side struts of Titty's pushchair which were the only bits she could reach, and stabilised it just before it seemed about to topple. She yelled as loud as she could, as much to control the crowd as the frantic woman, 'It's alright – the babies are all ok, it's alright.' The focus on their vulnerability, rather than their nuisance factor, helped instantly: a man was suddenly beside her shouting 'Give the girls some space, they have wains with them', and the knot of anxiety and fury around them seemed to loosen. Lee called out 'Thank you so much,' and made eye contact with everyone she could with as big a smile as she could muster, comforted by their conciliatory murmurs. She nodded vigorously and smiled rather than say anything more, thinking her English voice might make her sound like a soldier's wife which wouldn't help. Ariadne although she was shuddering had now stopped making any noise other than small whimpering sounds. Lee steered her fragile entourage back through the agitated pedestrians to a safe side street, took Finn from his chair for a cuddle and whispered reassurances, and thanked her lucky stars that Breff though now awake seemed unconcerned.

'So we came back, without buying a single thing,' Lee concluded her narration to Bruno, who was still at the flat when she got home. 'It was pretty scary, but they opened up the roadblock pretty soon. I don't know why Ariadne screamed like that, it made everything so much worse.'

'What about her kid?' Bruno asked.

'Titty didn't make a sound. Not a squeak out of her. The boys were both quiet too, I guess they were more curious than anything. I could see the soldiers were starting to drag the barriers back and were letting people filter through, but by then I just wanted to get home.'

'Doesn't sound like a bomb scare,' Bruno decided, '– they take a while to check out. More like a barney. The Tartan gangs throwing their weight around.'

'Oh yeah – I did see some tartan scarves, now you say that. I didn't think of that at the time – I thought they only came out when there was a football match. We'd deliberately avoided dole day too.'

'No such thing as safe days now.'

Bruno was cutting an emergency plectrum from a Marlborough packet. He finished his careful shaping before continuing his point: 'And it never is about the footie, except to get their timing. That ground is just the place the herd gathers, then they all leave together mob-handed and stampede down the Lisburn Road, slaughtering any random Mick rash enough to be on the streets. To them it's not so much a football stadium, more an unofficial paramilitary training ground. What shop were you heading for?'

'I thought C&A – Elaine said they sell Mary Quant stuff there,' Lee said, adding as they both knew even a pair of Mary Quant tights would be way beyond their budget, 'just to look, of course, and get ideas...' Bruno didn't even point out that the Sunday papers shared around their group were full of such ideas, but she was increasingly recognising how rash she'd been to submit to Ariadne's pleas, after Cara's warnings had kept her safe for weeks now. 'I'll stick to walks in the park and by the river, now,' she promised.

On Wednesday Bruno's time-table meant a tutorial all morning and lectures all afternoon, and he generally had a pint for his lunch in the Union bar. Lee often met him there in the early afternoon, after using the students' launderette in the morning, but this Wednesday she didn't feel like lugging a heap of washing through the bitter streets, nor did she feel like staying in, so she went round to see Dervla who lived very near the Union buildings.

Dervla's home was a big old house, crumbly and gritty on the outside, with a pillared porch from which grey plaster flaked thickly, littering the steep steps with pale debris from this once-grandiose portal. Inside, most of the house was bare. The front room contained a lot of sand, at one time an indoor sandpit but long since overflowing into the dust and fluff and random toys to create a strangely surreal landscape, with a headless doll featuring groggily as a diminutive Ozymandias. The living room, not used as such, was also bare apart from a maroon velvet chaise-longue with one foot missing which appeared, from the number of tools on the floor around it, in the process of being repaired. The kitchen was their only actual living-room, and was constantly exciting to Lee who had never occupied unfurnished premises and coveted the potential scope.

Here Dervla's exuberant personality and modernist aspirations were expressing themselves extensively and – to Lee – impressively. Dervla intermittently attended art college, where she was completing a vocational course started eight years and three children ago. Tom, her husband, worked for a Belfast newspaper but had hopes of going to London and becoming a journalist on a national paper. In the meantime, Dervla's ambition to complete her course held them in Belfast – ostensibly anyway, though Lee suspected it had also much to do with the immobilising poverty that kept so many in the city, shifting restlessly like iron filings in a magnetic experiment, to convince themselves they had a freedom of sorts.

Lee bumped the push-chair, backwards, up the steps with Breff, wide awake, giving a startled laugh at every jolt and Finn clambering ahead. Dervla was in, and welcomed them all, taking them directly into the kitchen where she was tie-dyeing some dungarees in the stone sink. Lee adored this room. Above the sink were shelves filled with the pottery made by Dervla herself and her art-student friends, and the walls were filled with big geometric murals in acrylic paint in what Dervla called 'Aztec' colours: yellow ochre, burnt sienna, and black. Tom had bought 'for practically nothing' a trestle table and two benches which he had cleaned and clear-varnished. The cupboards, all filled with artistic equipment and outcomes, had been similarly treated, with big black iron handles added. There was a wickerwork linen basket behind the door and a large urn used as a vase for huge sticks of honesty. Big cushions lay on the rather greasy tiled floor and there were several cat dishes, sitting amid the clutter of their scattered contents, under the table where Breff had promptly crawled.

Lee scooped him up and held him on her hip while she talked to Dervla, who managed to look successfully skinny even wearing a thick arran sweater of Tom's tucked inside her tight-fitting suede jeans. Lee was envious of her friend's figure, envious of her long straight hair, and envious of the talent and ingenuity she used to decorate her house on a blatant, bragging, shoestring. She was also very proud of this friendship.

Dervla plonked two mugs of coffee down on the table and went over to a large pottery jar labeled 'cookies' to fetch oatmeal biscuits for Finn and Tommy, successfully distracting her youngest son from eating the plasticine he had been holding.

'Did you make those things? Gosh, you are clever', Lee sighed ingenuously, wishing she was an art student living in a kitchen that looked like a studio, doing inventive things to old dungarees.

'Oh they're dead easy or I wouldn't be doing them,' said Dervla, handing Breff back so she could restore a leg to its bear owner and turn to a page in *The Animals Merry Christmas* that showed Richard Scarry's idea of a lion. She checked the softness of the apple-sized balls of plasticine quickly in her hand and gave them one each. 'No more biscuits till we have two nice lions roaring, now' she instructed, and sauntered back to the table, pushing her sleek hair over her shoulder and smoothing her hands on her self-made, self-designed jeans. 'So what's happening with you two, now?' she asked Lee as she reseated herself. 'Is Bruno playing at any new clubs?'

'I think he's mostly at Mick's Bar these days.' Lee's vagueness was genuine. Although proud of her husband's talent and pleased to be associated with it by proxy, her initial enthusiasm for Irish folk songs had waned recently, since so many of them seemed now like animated war-cries. She went along to the sessions when he played folk blues, but his audiences nowadays seemed mainly to prefer the traditional songs that told the stories of historical hostilities, usually laced with equally long standing profanities. Lee knew them all by heart.

Dervla looked at her curiously. 'You should go with him.'

'I do sometimes.'

'Well, up to you, Lee. I would be worried some wee bitch would get her claws into him.' Dervla was laughing but her eyes watched Lee intently.

Lee felt gratified at this image of the desirability of her husband, and thought suddenly, perhaps I have something Dervla envies, then. A good marriage. Dervla and Tom were rarely seen together, although they worked so hard on the house they shared. It's like a big weather house, Lee thought, as each used the other's presence or absence in it as their reason to go out or stay in, since one had to be there to 'mind' the children, although the two elder seemed to mind themselves pretty well in Lee's opinion. Bruno was in the habit of bringing his friends home after the club or a pub if Lee hadn't accompanied him there. Perhaps this was in its own way glamorous to Dervla? This exciting possibility sustained her self-esteem while she was shown Dervla's home-made Christmas candles – red and purple, some already sold to the gift shops in town – and her batik curtaining, and the evening dress she was making from an Edwardian stole she found in a jumble sale.

Lee usually left after her visits feeling daunted by the resourcefulness of her talented friend. But I have a talent too, Lee insisted to herself as she bumped the pushchair back down the steps to the street – I have a talent for people. At least I know that loving people and accepting them is what matters. Surely that's a kind of talent. The Belfast drizzle sleeted icily on her face as she turned her head to the wind.

In the Union bar, the group were passing around printed cards and posters with photographs with violent scenes of uniformed men with batons raised above unprotected heads, which she took to be from the infamous Burntollet march the year before. Below these images of cowering men and screaming women, the legend read TAKE A TRIP, LOOK AROUND — SEE THE PIGS THAT RUN OUR TOWN.

'Take some,' said the man holding the bundle of posters, 'Put them up on your lamp-post. Let the bastards know we won't be intimidated.'

Lee took one and looked to Bruno uncertainly. He said cheerily, 'Grand job, John, good man yourself,' and then quietly to Lee, not even looking at her, 'Put it in your bag.' Lee obeyed, and the man called John picked up his pint and said genially 'This your wee girl? I hope you're looking after her all right, now.' He was looking at her as he talked. 'English, if I'm not mistaken? Keen to see the real culture of our fair city, I'm sure. Well you won't see it in these mean streets. You should take her up to the Jubilee on a Friday, my lad.'

'Oh aye,' Bruno agreed heartily, making contact with Lee in the quick hard stare she knew meant to keep quiet, 'Good craic there, I'll be bound.'

'But you've not been,' the man called John persisted, 'You can't be showing her the city without a trip to the Jubilee. Why, it's the fire in the belly of the city, man – it's where the true story lies. Our past, our present, our fucking future!' He raised his Guinness pot above his head as he roared the last two words and there were several cheers from the group that surrounded them and re-claimed his attention.

Lee never stayed long if she had the children, even though no-one seemed to mind the pushchair in the corner, and this time Bruno came with her when she left to go home shortly afterwards. She asked Bruno what was going on with the posters.

'He wants us to decorate the streets with them. Great way to start a riot!'

'Why doesn't he send copies of the actual photographs to the newspapers? That would make more impact, surely. They were absolutely shocking – there was one little boy who looked petrified – and none of the marchers had any weapons. They were simply ambushed.'

'He did send them to the papers, they won't use them,' Bruno said simply, '– and by the way, those weren't taken in Burntollet last year, that's what's happening in Derry right now.'

'But that's terrible! That means everything is getting worse not better.'

Bruno scooped up Finn, who was tiring as Lee hadn't brought the pushchair seat that morning, and tucked him against his arm. 'Lee, you're right, but we're in a difficult place and we've children to protect. Don't play the heroine. That's all.'

When they had reached home, she tried again. 'Why is it OK to talk about these things in the bar but not in the street? There's more chance of being overheard in a bar, isn't there?'

'There is, but there's no-one there who would report you. Bars are tribal enclaves, Lee – you don't go in one unless you know everyone there is your tribe. There's Mick bars and Prod bars and student bars, they all have their codes and as long as you go in the right one, you're OK. Out in the street isn't so safe. It's all right for you – you're an English woman – you're safe on your own. But I'm Irish, and with long hair and hippy trousers – I have to watch myself when I'm moving around the town.'

Lee appreciated the lecture. She had known it all really, she reflected, just not in such clear terms. She pulled out the flyer, already dog-eared from her bag, and looked again at the shocking image.

'Who was the guy handing them out – you know him?'

'Yup. John's an anarchist. He's a friend of Michael Farrell – he's the quieter one, but he has more influence.'

Lee knew the second name: Michael Farrell had been in the news as leader of the Peoples' Democracy, Ulster's brief attempt at a cross-religious political group, the budding shoots of which had been mashed to a pulp on the day of the march that she had thought the photographs showed. And this was going on right now.

'Cheer up, love' said Bruno, 'I'll make us both a coffee. And I'll do bedtime tonight.'

Lee managed a bleak smile of appreciation. It wasn't even his turn.

'And if you really want to see more of John, I could ask him along to our next session. But watch out, I could see he took a shine to you.'

The idea of being admired by this charismatic stranger had not occurred to Lee, and she found it immediately irresistible. Besides, Dervla had said she should go out more with her husband, hadn't she? She would invite Melissa to tea on Thursday and ask her to bring her books and stay on, so she could go with Bruno to the folk night. Another benefit of living in such a convivial community!

6

ELSEWHERE IN THE CITY

DERVLA was right, Lee decided as she sat with the group at Mick's Bar – the usual 'cast of thousands' as Bruno would say when he couldn't remember who exactly from their known crowd had attended. Melissa had once explained to her that human friendship groups were rather like vacuoles, which are membrane-bound organelles which have no basic shape or size as their structure varies according to the requirements of the cell they inhabit. Lee was fascinated and had memorised both terms, feeling that as people are all merely collections of cells, this must somehow be relevant to every theory of life on the planet. Now, without exactly remembering any of the terminology, Lee was feeling there was something in the notion as they all merged together in the old parlour by the fire.

Throw on another, someone suggested, and the blaze rallied as the log jostled the embers. Josh and Bruno had been playing off and on for the last couple of hours, Bruno leading the singing and Josh adding nifty bass lines while others joined in randomly on fiddle, squeezebox, spoons, and tankard-on-table rhythm. It had been a good session. Even a banjo had joined them for a while. Now it was way into lock-in time and the music was becoming desultory.

John had accepted Bruno's invitation to join them, and was by now on the floor propped against the wall, chugging a beer and sucking on a bedraggled roll-up. He looked up at Bruno.

'Very nice. Very nice. But if you want to hear some real Irish folk songs, you should come with me tomorrow night –

you too, Lee. You'll be my guests.

Bruno took his capo off his guitar and picked up the case, shaking some slopped beer off the fabric. 'We've been singing "real Irish folk songs", John, all night.'

John started to heave himself to his feet, waving away various nearby hands moving to help him. His system seemed at first uncertain of success but eventually he achieved a perpendicular pose and launched into his reply to Bruno.

'Milk and water, lad, milk and water. I like a song with fire in its belly. And so should you, man – you have the voice, where's your fire?'

Lee, like the others, was gathering up all her outerwear for leaving, and listening intently to the subtext of the conversation. It seemed to be becoming interesting.

'So where do we go for these fire-bellied songs?' Bruno enquired cautiously.

John waited for a few moments until most of the group were gone, and only Bruno and herself remained.

Then he said 'Down the Markets.'

Lee was immediately curious. None of their group went near the Markets. When she'd woken in the night to the sound of gunfire, Bruno had generally soothed her by saying, 'It's coming from the Markets. It's just… the Markets.'

'Where in the Markets?' Bruno's query sounded more uncertain than dismissive.

'Jubilee Arms. You wouldn't know it. Not your kind of place.'

'So… why would I go there?'

John was still smiling. He clapped Bruno on the back as he answered 'For the songs, man! I'm willing to bet you'll hear a few there you've not heard before.'

He pitched the stub of his roll-up into the fire and headed for the door. As he passed Lee, he patted her on the head. "Don't worry, pet. You'll be fine. You'll be with me.'

He turned to Bruno as if it was all sorted and agreed now.

'Tomorrow evening, then,' he said. 'Seven o'clock – be ready. I'll pick you up in front of the shop. ' And before either of them had time to collude in any demurral, he left them, calling behind him 'You'll hear the real stuff, man – songs of the struggle, alive and fuckin' kicking. It's not done yet Bruno – it never will be. Never.'

Later, Lee was still not quite sure how it had happened. True, term was nearly over for Bruno but she wasn't used to two such late nights in succession, and they had never really said yes, and it would mean asking Melissa to sit once again as she was the only one on close call – yet somehow or other, when they heard the taxi hoot in the main street outside shortly after seven, Lee and Bruno were both ready and waiting. Lee had taken the chance to wear her green duffle coat, which she had reluctantly reconsigned to serve as a blanket some time ago but was the warmest outerwear she had. Bruno signalled from the window and they clattered down the back stairs and got in the back.

The driver twisted in his seat to look at them and then turned back to McGuffin in the shotgun seat to ask dubiously 'Are ye sure you want the Jubilee, now?'

'Sure as I'm going to be pissed by closing time,' was the genial reply.

The driver let out the clutch and moved off, muttering 'Well, it's your funeral.'

Lee and Bruno in the back exchanged looks of exaggerated trepidation and Lee grabbed Bruno's hand. 'He sounds like Eeyore,' she whispered, to see if he would smile. He didn't smile, but he did hold her hand throughout the journey.

The Markets were fairly deserted at this hour, with day's business done and the evening's activity not yet underway. Street lighting was patchy, and Lee noticed it looked as if the lamps had been used for target practice. Lee shivered: it all looked like a set for a film noir, with the shuttered doors and windows, angry graffiti, and debris everywhere. If the silent alleys and side streets could speak, she thought, they'd be saying 'What the fuck are you playing at? Stay in the taxi and leave while you still can'.

The Jubilee stood on the corner of one of those inaudibly threatening side streets. John had the driver's cash ready to give him before anyone opened a door, then said 'OK, you two, out the car, in the door and up the stairs. Move!'

Bruno and Lee moved. The stairs were just inside the door of the pub, so at least they didn't have to go through the crowd at the bar, who were clearly aware of them hurtling past, as they had all turned suddenly silent. Lee became belatedly aware that her Englishness was half their problem. No longer were they in terrain where her nationality made her a neutral figure in what was primarily a local territorial dispute – this was the real thing, an ancient history of visceral hatred, and she tried to slow her breathing to suppress the rising, belated, sense of panic. Bruno appeared to be doing his best to look like a Catholic, but success here would be unlikely. Both of them stayed close to John as he strode confidently up the stairs and led them into the function room, a longish, narrow, space with a stage at the far end and rows of hard-back chairs on either side. Lee was surprised to see it was nearly full already, and relieved that they were met by cries of greeting.

'How you doing John?'

'How's about you, man?'

'John! Good to see you'

These and other greetings sounded around them, and Lee was relieved to note that the speakers' glances included herself and Bruno, with slight nods extended to further reassure them. John was responding cheerily to each of them, with like familiarity,

'Ah, I'm grand, Tommo. Stickin' out, boyo. Good to see you, man…'

Lee watched as people stood and stretched out over heads of others to shake his hand. She was impressed. Bruno, she noticed, was making very sure they weren't separated from him by any of these well-wishers as they made their way along the hall. John, she realised now, was heading for three seats together about halfway up the hall, which he successfully claimed. Lee felt more relaxed once they were settled down, and started to look around the audience.

She wasn't sure what she'd been expecting after the hype from the taxi driver, and then the way they'd been watched as they hurried up the stairs, but this audience all looked like ordinary people. Couples, small groups, the odd man on his own. Well, some of them, a few, were a bit hard looking... a couple of them looked like they were looking quietly around too... Her eyes met another gaze, steady and unwavering. She quickly dropped her head and fussed with the toggle of her duffle coat.

'You OK?' Bruno asked quietly.

She nodded, then whispered, "Don't look, but there's some tough guys in here.'

'I won't look,' Bruno promised, 'And don't you look at them either. Seriously. Do Not Look.'

'I'm not.' she breathed.

There was a semblance of hush in the front rows then as someone, presumably the emcee of the event, emerged with his hands out, calling for hush. He had to call several times more before this was even remotely achieved, because every promised aspect of the great night they were going to have – except the reminder they had to go down to the bar for their drinks – inspired a rousing cheer. Eventually the build-up was high enough for him to wave on the guests of the night and four men bounded on stage double-pumping their fists and yelling 'Erin go Bragh'. The audience yelled back with other rebel slogans, drumming their feet on the board floor.

'You had to pity the poor sods in the bar downstairs,' Bruno said later, 'It must've been like having your head inside a Lambeg drum.'

Bruno was enjoying reliving the entire event to Elaine when she came over next evening. Lee was impressed by his recall, which was far more detailed than hers after several shots from John's whiskey flask, and he painted a vivid picture of a sequence that had become a bit of a blur to her.

'So then the boyos grabbed their stuff – they had a couple of guitars, a banjo and a fiddle – and they they tore into The Rising of the Moon, giving it some stick and taking no prisoners.'

'Did you sing along?' Elaine wanted to know.

'Everyone did! They were hammering out all the old rebel songs, and everyone knew the choruses. Most seemed to know all the verses, too. So that was basically how it went on all night – a tirade of anti-Brit, anti-army, anti-police, anti-Unionist, anti-Free-Stater songs, and the audience stamping and screaming and practically foaming at the mouth.'

Elaine's eyes were wide. 'I'd love to have seen that – like a part of history.'

Bruno nodded. 'You could say that all right, but I fear it's a history still in the making. Seriously, Elaine, it's not over yet. These boyos are dyed-in-the-wool United-Ireland fanatics. A twenty-six-county Free State and a six-county North under Brit rule doesn't cut any ice with them. Border? Fuck your border! And fuck all those arse-licking Quislings – De Valera and his bunch of wankers who caved in to the Brits and accepted the partition. They still see it as carving up Kathleen ni Houlihan's own darlin' Emerald Isle.'

'Seriously? You think some of them still feel that strongly? I mean, Partition was nearly fifty years ago – surely only the very old guard still even remember it?'

Bruno was both shaking his head and nodding at Elaine's point. Lee was both impressed and envious of this feat as she felt that if she had attempted any such manoeuvre her head would have fallen off.

'I'm telling you, this one could've started a new rebellion

right then and right there, – song of the night, for me, I'll not forget that chorus.'

And he sang:

'Take it down from the mast, Irish traitors,

It's the flag the Republicans claim.

It can never belong to Free Staters,

For you brought on it nothing but shame!'

Then he added to Lee, 'G, C, G, – D, C, D, G. Very easy chords.'

Despite her hangover, Lee felt touched by this information. Bruno was theoretically teaching Lee to play guitar, but it was so rarely out in someone else's hands that this hadn't progressed beyond the Dubliners version of *The Wild Rover*, which had similar simplicity. Every now and again he remembered, and she always felt a frisson of pride and pleasure at this continuing connection with his world.

Elaine had looked anxiously towards the window, but Lee knew their sound was muffled to the outside by the towels laid along the inner sill to sop up the daily frost-melt She raised a limp hand vaguely and made a movement as near as a nod as her head would allow, and Elaine looked relieved. Bruno continued.

'So the front man – I don't remember the name of the group, do you Lee? Ah well, we won't see them on posters round here anyway – he proudly announced that they'd sung it last week in a pub in Dundalk and been summarily ejected! A sort of honour for them – 'Suffering For The Cause' and all that, but it does show that some of the Free State folk are not as keen as the boys of the Belfast Markets are to put the clock back!'

'Dominic Behan, wasn't it, that one?' said Elaine, and Lee nodded. She knew a fair few of the words, at least of the version the Dubliners had recorded back in the '60s, when people like her had no idea they were listening to living history, but she hadn't dared raise her voice with the chanting crowd on the previous night. She knew these were tribal battle cries in a foreign country. She had mouthed along with her neighbours and hoped she wasn't secretly under surveillance. It wasn't only the hard-faced watchers who scared her: she and Bruno and John were sitting right in the eye-line of two men in fawn raincoats in the back row. These two had attracted some ribaldry from the crowd, and Lee had been meaning to ask Bruno about it, so she was pleased he was now weaving their presence into his narrative.

'… couple of Special Branch boys,' he was saying, 'Right behind us! It was obvious the audience knew they were there, and the group knew too, and the SB men knew we all knew, but it seemed like there was a kind of unofficial truce happening – maybe just for the gig, who knows? They might have nabbed the lads as soon as they'd packed their gear and started leaving.'

Elaine, like Lee, had been in Belfast long enough to know the 'Special Branch' of the Royal Ulster Constabulary was dedicated to combating the IRA and worked with MI5 and army Intelligence. Her eyes widened as Bruno carried on with his dramatic retelling evening's unspoken subtext.

'Whatever the facts of it, the group made plenty of cracks about those two guys, and the two guys just sat there, grinning a bit from time to time. The audience never got riled by them, not even those hard-faced flat-eyed guys dotted around. Not last night, anyways. Tomorrow, who knows.'

'What a tale,' said Elaine, impressed. Bruno picked up his guitar and shifted the capo so he could strum the chords of that Civil Rights Movement protest song made famous by Pete Seeger: *We Shall Overcome*. He sang the opening words, saying in midline to Lee 'You can do this one, you know, simples – C, F, G7, you want to?'

Lee shook her head, but carefully. 'Tomorrow?'

Bruno continued to chord, almost in a reverie, as he finished his saga.

'I'll never forget the finish of the night, either. The whole audience on its feet, the group lined up front stage, everybody giving a Black Power salute as we sang.'

He ended his story with the song, and at 'Deep in my heart, I do believe,' Elaine joined in with him and they both sang together, 'We shall overcome one day.'

There was a haunting moment of silence. Bruno had recreated the whole evening so well that Lee felt near to tears of emotion all over again. She remembered now how he had whispered to her as they sang those familiar words 'Well, sweetheart, there's our peace anthem going down the bloody drain.'

John had hustled them out to the waiting taxi, and as she stumbled out Lee had asked him, naively, 'Is it always like that?' and he'd laughed so hard she thought he'd have a fit. She remembered his lupine grin as they parted, and him calling after them, as Bruno steered her towards their back gate, 'Fuckin' great night, eh?'

Bruno was saying it again now. 'We sweated buckets, but we had a fucking great time.'

'I don't remember', mourned Lee, 'They'd spiked that booze with alcohol, my head's a rattling bucket and I wish it would go away. I don't remember anything.'

But she did remember the camaraderie, and the frisson of the final defiant song, and that deep and extraordinary sense of being part of something primitive and frightening but profound and precious too. Even as her head pounded Lee knew that beyond the barriers of prejudice, something real and valuable was fighting for survival, and it seemed to her that 'something' was not a culture or a creed but sheer human spirit. *We shall overcome*, she murmured as she moved to the kitchen to make another black coffee, *We shall overcome some day,* and the mantra somehow seemed to ease the ache.

'The main thing that stays with me though, now the euphoria – sort of – has all gone, is realising that it's... ' Lee's voice halted. Melissa waited inquisitively. They were walking back from the park, having taken advantage of a burst of bitter sunshine, and they had to keep stopping as Finn squatted suddenly to examine treasures like a fallen leaf caught in a web. He walked fast when on the move again, so their journey had a strange staccato rhythm which their chat seemed to have unconsciously absorbed.

'It?' prompted Melissa.

Lee nodded without clarifying, deep in her own thoughts. 'I knew it was ingrained and historical, I knew it could be irrational and violent; but It's much more complex than that.' She became aware of Melissa's interrogative expression. 'I mean, this hostility, it's not just anti-Prod and anti-English, but anti-anyone who accepts the border – even if they're Catholic.'

'A minority are like that,' Melissa suggested, 'In terms of the population, a small minority.'

'It doesn't feel like small when you're smaller,' Lee asserted earnestly, 'And when you're in the middle you can almost smell the rage… it's more than that, it's something deadly. They're like plague cells aren't they? I mean, as individuals they're harmless nuts but if they all got together for anything more than a sing-song, they could really infect the community. I've always wondered why the guys in Stormont have never done anything more positive about integration – I mean, obviously they can't do mixed housing estates, that wouldn't be safe, but maybe jobs? insisting you had to have a mix at work.'

Melissa laughed. 'Lee, you know they're all bigots. They wouldn't have got their posts if they weren't!'

They reached Mr Smith's newsagents.

'You coming up?' Lee enquired, and Melissa said that her thesis was calling so she'd just give Lee a hand up the stairs and then pootle off. Finn clambered up ahead and Lee held Breff, as the pushchair needed to be half-retracted to manage the stairwell corner. As the two women deftly completed the familiar manoeuvre and reached their door, with Melissa steadying everything so the door could open without knocking it all back down the steps, Lee was assailed with a feeling of anticipated loss. We'll have to leave, she thought with sudden, overwhelming, prescience: I really believed I had something to offer here, but I can't see how it can ever get through the miasma of mistrust in this ossified city. If it can't munch me whole, it'll just spit me out.

'Cheer up Lee, we've nearly reached the solstice,' Melissa told her by way of farewell as she descended, 'everything will seem better soon.'

7

DO THEY KNOW IT'S CHRISTMAS

'DID YOU KNOW James keeps going on about that wife-swapping party?' said Cara next day as they both drank coffee in the chaotic living-room of Lee and Bruno's flat. The fire had been on all day and, though ineffective to defeat the chilliness in the air, it had now combined with Cara's cigarette smoke to create a choky dryness.

This had been Lee's afternoon to look after Samantha, and Cara was now collecting her after a session of Christmas shopping. Their child-sharing system was especially useful now that random road-blocks from the British soldiers were causing traffic jams and further chaos across the town, but Lee had found her session with all three children strenuous that day, and the cold outside seemed to pervade the living room with malevolent bleakness. Their cumbersome fireguard, permanently erected and extended to protect the children from the electric fire, reminded her of a cage, and every time a toy clanged against it the sound jarred her. Samantha's fretful mood had improved unexpectedly just before her mother returned, and now both the mobile children were engrossed in a game called 'tall giraffes' which consisted of chasing each other around the mattress-sofa until the next giggling collision. Lee had investigated Cara's purchases, agreed on the expense of Christmas, deplored the weather, and now they sat with their coffee mugs at the tail end of a December afternoon, each waiting for it to be time to get the tea, get the children off to bed, and wait for the return of the men and the start of the evening. And now, Cara was asking, perhaps idly, perhaps maliciously, if she was aware that James was talking about a wife-swapping party.

'What wife-swapping party?' asked Lee.

'He says that you and Bruno suggested we all got together some time for a wife-swapping party.' Cara hunted round for her cigarettes and looked enquiringly at Lee.

'Oh, that. I made some daft joke about it at Gary's do. I'd forgotten.'

'Well, James is serious. Fionnula is furious.'

'I suppose she would be, if they're only just married and he keeps going on about shagging someone else.' Lee felt a little depressed at the thought of the hostility she had somehow unwittingly provoked. She was also, as always, piqued by the hints that Cara so frequently proffered of a friendship with James and Fionnula which was deeper than their own. The two couples were apparently frequent co-visitors, but Cara was always evasive in advance, belatedly revealing details in a way Lee found bafflingly calculated. Lee and Cara met practically daily now, and there was an intimacy between them that seemed so close as to be nearly complete, except for these contrived omissions. 'I must be going now, I've got a pile of work to do at home,' Cara would say, and then reveal at their next meeting that her work had in fact been preparing a meal for James and Fionnula. Lee always felt vaguely hurt, as she could see no reason for the secrecy or Cara's sly air of retrospective triumph. So her relationship with Cara remained curiously unstable, and on Lee's side curiously dependent. She needed this to last. She had attained her friend's confidence and affection once before and somehow lost it, and she desperately wanted not to lose it again. So she simply looked slightly downcast at Cara's hints of private talks with James and Fionnula, and said nothing.

'Well,' said Cara, gathering her bags and parcels, 'Your turn next. Did you say you're doing your Christmas shopping on Thursday?'

'Yes, Bruno's not working and we thought we'd go together.'

'Well you can leave the baby at our place too, he's no bother and you'll get on better. You're better not to have the pushchair down the town, there was another bomb scare at Marks' today and I wasn't allowed in the door. I'd hate to be caught in a panic with a pushchair.'

Lee nodded shudderingly, remembering her last attempt at a trip uptown. With Bruno there would be little time spent in the big shops and none of it browsing, but it would be nice to have a morning off together. Samantha was buttoned protestingly into her coat, tied into her knitted mitts and bonnet, and Cara departed.

When Thursday arrived and Lee had handed over the children and shared a coffee with Cara, she came home to find Bruno was engrossed in working out the chords to *Albatross* from a Fleetwood Mac single he'd borrowed from Josh, and clearly not in a shopping mood. Lee was quite happy to use the time with her own private preparations. She was making egg cosies to represent the three kings and the shepherds, using scraps of coloured felt and a black marker pen. Though whether we'll ever need six boiled eggs at Christmas, or even Easter, is doubtful, Lee thought, but she continued contentedly with her project until suddenly remembering she needed to get potatoes for supper. Maybe some veg too, she thought, and to save time decided to go to the local greengrocers just a couple of minutes down the road rather than one of the cheaper shops further away.

There was only one person waiting to be served: an Indian-looking lady who was asking repeatedly for okra. The woman in the shop stared at her. Lee looked around the sacks of potatoes and cabbages, with peppers the most exotic looking vegetable in sight, and wondered how the Indian-looking lady was coping with life in Ireland.

'Ladies fingers?' Lee suggested but the woman behind the counter looked more confused than ever. She was pointing at all the sacks on view in turn, including the apples, but the Indian lady equally silently shook her head at them all. Eventually she amended her suggestion to courgettes. Lee, who had been helpfully finger-miming small vegetables, now widened her air-grasp to courgette size, and the greengrocer pointed hopefully to the cucumbers. The Indian lady shook her head at these, and at the parsnips and the leeks and at the boiled beetroot.

By now she was looking sad and Lee, as interpreter, was at a loss, and the woman behind the counter decided it was time to speak. She leaned across the counter and said loudly and carefully: 'Vegetable man no come today.'

The Indian lady thanked her and departed. Lee handed over sixpence for her bag of potatoes, took her change and left the shop gasping with stifled mirth, not remembering until she got home she'd forgotten to get any greens. 'Just chips and beans for supper,' she called out to Bruno, 'Vegetable man no come today.'

Lee was still giggling as she recounted her story, but Bruno looked sombre. "That's the insularity that's at the heart of it, Lee,' he said, 'and we laugh, because it's funny, but the bigotry that's breeding there will kill us if we don't wise up.'

That night the late news on the tranny reported a man had been shot dead in his home in West Belfast. 'Police believe this was a crime of attempted robbery which was thwarted,' said the report, adding that Mr Jardin was a managing director and a member of the Orange Lodge and was well known as a keen gun collector.

'Let's pray to god they do the trenches thing and have a ceasefire next week for Christmas' said Bruno, as he switched the radio off.

Christmas was only just over a week away now, and had become an imminent awareness. More than a season or an event, it seemed almost a entity in itself, given life by their every reference like an inflatable paddling pool growing slowly with each panted breath until something solid and complete is created. Like dragging an inflatable genie from a magic lamp, they created an atmosphere of excitement of anticipation by their own urgent need for it to exist. Something colourful and glittering simply had to shine through the murky darkness of a Belfast winter: it glowed with their own reflected desire. 'What are you doing at Christmas?' every caller asked, as the clammy chill outside encircled them and the word itself became an amulet for survival against the overwhelming grimness.

The first definite step in the celebrations for Lee and Bruno was the Chinese meal foursome on Friday. This was to be the official Christmas meal for Cara and Paul, since Paul had succeeded in getting part-time work as a night porter and would be working through Christmas nights and sleeping through what was left of the days after his double shift. Lee and Bruno had more festivities to look forward to: they were going to Melissa's for a pre-Christmas dinner, and celebrating the day itself in their own flat. They had evaded invitations from Bruno's family in Donegal with explanations of the difficulty of journeying with two young children.

They intended to create their own perfect Christmas idyll. Lee planned to make mince pies and other seasonal treats and Bruno had announced his intention to buy ten pounds worth of drink for the holiday. An enormous investment it seemed to them all. Everyone had promised to call on their way to or from their duty-trips to relations, everybody promised to bring something, as Christmas, unbearably slow like in childhood days, approached.

The Chinese meal was a disappointment to Lee. The meal itself was quite nice, but a desultory conversation on the responsibilities of parenthood had developed into something approaching acrimonious disagreement. Lee was enlarging at some length, as she not infrequently did, on the importance of never inhibiting the emerging personality of the growing child. Paul, perhaps a little bored, interrupted.

'Come off it, Lee, it doesn't really matter a shit, does it?'

'What do you mean Paul? Of course it does!'

'Oh balls. Look, you've got all these ideas about encouraging kids and listening to them and not thumping them – well, all right, so did I at first. But when it comes down to it, they can all be wee shites. So we thump them. Well, does it matter? We got thumped by our parents, who never listened to us, and OK you resent it like hell when you're a kid but, face it, we've all come out all right so they didn't do too badly for us, so we're not going to do any harm by doing the same things to our kids.'

Lee stared appalled.

'I don't agree with any of that, Paul. I don't think we should give up trying to do our best just because our parents didn't manage it, that's exactly what's wrong with our whole society! The young see the flaws but then when they're old enough to do things differently, they start to rationalise acceptance of the whole rotten system.'

'I'm not rationalising any fucking thing' said Paul annoyedly. 'I'm just saying Samantha is a wee shite and she needs thumped, and when I was her age I was probably a wee shite who needed thumping. And I got it – and I've survived, haven't I?'

Lee transferred her frustrated gaze to Bruno.

'Do you agree with that?' she demanded.

'Not a word, but I'm not going to argue about it,' he responded, and they ordered coffee.

'You are still coming tonight, aren't you?' Melissa asked next afternoon when Lee called round. 'It's just a little pre-Christmas dinner for my favourite people. That's you two and another couple you haven't met – at least, I don't think you have. They're fabulous! Well, he's fabulous, she's rather sweet. Can you bring some records?'

'What sort do you want? I should think so, but they're mainly ones we've borrowed so we'll have to be pretty careful with them.' People tended to bring their records round to play to Bruno, and Bruno tended to say 'Can I hold onto that for a few days?' so they had quite a collection.

'Well, nothing too folksy.'

'Old Beatles? They're lovely and Christmassy. I'm really looking forward to tonight, Melissa, I love parties.'

Lee stretched on the floor of Melissa's living room, conscious of a specific cause for her sense of luxury. She decided in this instance it was located in the absence of children. It wasn't a good flat to bring children. It was actually rather a strange flat, and seemed completely unsuited to Melissa's personality. Not even an entire flat, it was one room in an apartment belonging to a university lecturer with whom Melissa was having one of her ambivalent and intense relationships. The flat had been furnished and decorated in a way the landlord considered suitable for the affluent tastes of the kind of tenants his rent had in mind, so there was a profusion of teak with gilt handles and black PVC upholstery. There was also a cocktail bar, which served Melissa as a second bookcase. The mauve and scarlet wallpaper, thickly crusted with fleur-de-lys, also seemed designed to create an atmosphere of idle alcoholic indulgence rather than academic industry. Amidst the slick plastic fittings, Melissa had installed a piano which she announced she would learn to play as an antidote to research. Erotic posters now nearly obliterated the walls, and three small electric fires burned steadily from their sentinel posts on top of piles of books and papers and on the record player. Melissa worried, somewhat unrealistically, Lee considered, about singeing the carpet.

Melissa produced a bottle of red wine from the evening's stock.

'I shouldn't drink, really' said Lee, 'I'm on antibiotics.'

'Oh dear. What's wrong with you?'

'Oh, just the same old stuff. Sinuses, and that. It's probably all psychosomatic anyway, in this bloody place. Breff still keeps being sick, you know – in fact Siobhan says all the children in her area keep being sick. Or diarrhoea. One or the other or both. I asked the doctor if it could be the CS gas, but he just laughed and said CS gas never hurt anyone. Bloody liar, they used to say on the radio about it – 'taken to hospital suffering effects of CS gas,' but they've stopped them from saying that now. They still use it though.'

'But the effects would only be from direct contact, surely?' said Melissa, giving up the search for a corkscrew and ramming the cork down into the bottle with a fork – 'I've nothing to give you to eat, you know me, always watching my weight.'

'That's ok, I wouldn't eat anyway as we're having a meal tonight. Yes, it would be direct contact for them to be taken to hospital like that, but if you think about it, Belfast is in a valley and the air is never totally clear, and it's not that big a city for any area to be able to avoid it completely. The stuff hangs around in the atmosphere and comes down when it rains. I always feel worse on Sundays, because Friday and Saturday are riot nights when they belt the stuff into the air and then on Sunday it rains. Why do we even wonder why we feel so grotty.'

'Hangover?' suggested Melissa, reseating herself on the floor beside Lee and pouring red wine into two mugs.

Lee conceded the point. 'Anyway', she said, 'I'm looking forward to tonight. I love parties.'

'So do I. Except those hothouse ones, when everyone's traumas seem to blossom and bloom.'

'I haven't noticed party times being any more traumatic than any other times,' Lee said, 'I mean, we're a pretty hung-up lot even at the best of times.'

'Well, parties seem to release it all. I know I get overwrought and then terribly down if I don't get the man I'm after. It makes me get quite bitchy.'

Lee could not imagine the Melissa she saw, sexy and serene, succumbing to negativity by failing to 'get the man she was after' so she laughed.

'Well, I suppose as we're all just animals, our most basic instinct is to mate,' she said. 'Humans are no different from any other life form. Koalas, or snakes, or spiders!'

'Some spiders eat each other,' said Melissa.

'Well, you know what I mean. Humans are just a tribe – we may be a big one but there's less of us than locusts.' She paused as Melissa was looking as if she might fetch an encyclopaedia, and although locusts groups were plagues, were there actually many of them around? 'Ants, anyway.' she amended.

'Worms,' said Melissa energetically. 'Worms are massively the biggest species – parasitic ones particularly. Roundworms!'

'Exactly.' Lee preferred not to reflect too deeply on the overwhelming prevalence of roundworms so she continued with her thesis: 'Humans aren't the apex of the creatures, we're just the most vocal. We've got this ability to develop language, and that makes us storytellers and creatives of all kinds, but it's sent us crazy too. We need to understand we have to connect or we'll end up destroying each other.'

'Natural culling?' suggested Melissa.

Lee shook her head. 'But it isn't natural, here, it's arbitrated by hatred, and we don't need a cull – we could all get along. We have all the skills we need to co-operate.'

'If you're talking about animals, Lee, then fighting for control of territory is as natural as mating.' Melissa said. 'And we all need that. Speaking of which, who's going to be at your place on The Day? Anyone I don't know?'

She seemed determined to move the tempo to more languorous, semi-erotic, converse so Lee lay with her on the floor, drinking red wine without food so as not to get fat, and musing on men in general and particular.

'I just love dancing,' Lee said finally, 'I love getting pissed and making an exhibition of myself dancing in crazy ways. I used to think it was all therapeutic, you know, after having to keep so much of myself contained during the week when I'm looking after the children, tuning into their needs all the time, not my own. I used to think it was all a essential release of suppressed tension. But now I think perhaps I'm just the kind of shallow-minded person who likes dancing and getting pissed and making an exhibition of themselves.'

Melissa leapt to deny Lee's shallow-mindedness. Lee liked the denial, but still felt she was being realistic about her limitations. In fact, it seemed rather to confirm her suspicion of her own shallowness that she took such pleasure in hearing its refutation.

'Anyway,' she said eventually, 'I think people should touch more. We don't do it enough – we're all starved of tactile contact. Look at animals, they sniff each other all over, we have to confine our touching to whatever society deems appropriate, like shaking hands and holding babies, and then as soon as people get pissed or high, the barriers come down and all that held-back touching is irresistible. Our parties are like remedial touch-teaching sessions, everyone lolling on each others' knees and legs listening to records or singing, and people like us snogging with anyone who seems to fancy us. It's just ordinary physical touch we're starving for really, only we don't even recognise that – we locate our desire as sexual because that's what society has trained us to expect, so every touch encounter becomes sexual whether that's what we really need or not.'

Melissa demurred.

'I know I need sexual encounters. Touching is all very well and snogging is fine, but I always want it to end up in bed.'

'It's different for you, Melissa. With me, everyone keeps going on about what a great guy Bruno is, and they never do anything in the end.'

'Would you want them to?'

Lee was not sure. It was nice to have men holding you and yearning for more, and she liked the safe feeling when they reminded her of the impossibility of what they claimed to want. Lee's sexual enjoyment, which was intense, came from the excitement of provoking desire, but she felt her inability to prove personal fulfilment would be seen as inadequacy. In the aftermath of casual love-making, when so many of the men she met seemed to take refuge from self-doubt by contempt for their partners, she shrank from making herself vulnerable by revealing her private limitations. Even with Bruno, she liked the cuddling more, which was one of the reasons she felt non-possessive: if men liked to provoke noisy orgasms, the man she loved should have that chance too.

'I do like the idea of an open marriage,' she admitted, 'I mean, logically it's an essential element in a free community. People want long-term commitment for the children's sake, but it shouldn't limit anyone's personal life explorations.'

'Open – how? open to anyone? open all hours?' Melissa was laughing at her – no, just smiling. It had sounded for a moment like a jeer. Or even a sneer.

'You know what I mean,' said Lee, smiling herself and determined to recover that precious sense of womanly intimacy.

'So you wouldn't mind if Bruno shagged me, for instance?' Melissa was beaming. She seemed satisfied with Lee's small smile of assent.

'But what would Bruno think if you did go the whole way with someone?' Melissa persisted.

'I honestly don't think he'd mind. We've always liked doing different things at parties, even before we were married. He used to take his guitar and sing – it was all Clancey Brothers then – and I'd get bored and pissed and amorous and end up snogging some guy and when it was time to go, he'd come and break us up, probably scrounge a fag off the bloke, and take me home. And I'd probably be sick or something, and he'd always look after me.'

Lee contemplated for a moment the strange pattern of their courtship. 'I think actually he was usually glad to get me off his back. I suppose my ideal would have been a relationship in which we were aware of each other all the time, like an invisible thread secretly connecting us. But he's not like that and I came to realise if our relationship was going to last, it needed some other formula than interdependence. I'm still trying, really. The children are immensely fulfilling of course, they're amazing, but I don't want to be over possessive. I'd like to have lots of different relationships with loads of different people, and learn something from them all, wouldn't that be ideal?'

Melissa took another drink of wine and did not answer.

Lee, as she often did when discoursing, now started wondering whether she agreed with herself about what she'd just said. She decided she did. 'In fact,' she went on, 'the best thing about my marriage with Bruno is that it changes.. I've never been bored in this relationship.'

Lee spoke sincerely: this seemed to her significant and valuable. A meaningful relationship, in Lee's view, would never become static. Later she was to wonder whether variety had been an appropriate criterion of meaningfulness in marriage. *Only connect*, she later quoted to herself, wondering how, and when, she had forgotten that.

The dinner party that night was not a total success. 'You two couples are my favourite people in all Belfast', Melissa had said, and being so excessively fond of them both perhaps she had expected them to make an intuitive leap through unfamiliarity and to love each other too. Both couples, maybe a little jealous of this division in Melissa's affection, appeared slightly wary and on edge. As they were in different social circles it was difficult to keep the conversation general, and alcohol instead of blurring distinctions seemed to aggravate the polarities. During the meal Lee had tried to recapture the feeling of intimacy by talking about her childhood. This was usually irresistible to Melissa, who listened bird-eyed and alert, nodding encouragement and making sympathetic noises, while Lee relived tensions with her mother and the corrosive guilt of her mother's reproaches, and recounted how she had always competed with her brother for maternal love, and always despairingly failed. This time the formula didn't seem to be working: Melissa's usual encouraging indulgence was not forthcoming.

'Lee, you keep going on about trying to win your mother's

love, how jealous you were of your brother because she loved him more. It's actually the other way round, isn't it? I think it was your brother's love you wanted, and you were jealous of your mother because he loved her more than he loved you!'

Lee kept her smile bright but she felt herself tense with annoyance at Melissa and her breath quickened with apprehension.

'It wasn't like that, actually –'

'Come off it Lee. You're savagely jealous of her still, every time you talk about her it shows. Why do you think you married Bruno? He's the ideal brother for you, and your mother will never win him away!'

'Yeah, and the incest is great,' Bruno quipped blithely. Melissa's intense tone, contradicting the jocularity of her smile, had caused a frisson of embarrassment around the table, and Bruno's response had salvaged the moment with confident ease. Lee knew by his tight smile he was exasperated with Melissa and annoyed by her analysis, but everyone laughed, relieved, and the conversation turned to easier things. The candles were burning low, they needed changing for safety's sake. Were there more? A hunt ensued, and proved successful, but Lee was left with a feeling of distaste, and pique at Melissa's insistence. Of course Melissa knew it wasn't like that so why had she invented that response, and flung it at her in front of everyone? Lee felt bewildered and betrayed. She sat quiet till the end of the meal and after the curry plates were cleared away and wine passed round again, Melissa suggested they danced. This too seemed to highlight the intrinsic awkwardness of the encounter. There were three girls and only two men, and Bruno evidently did not want to dance with the rather plump upper-middle-class girl who was Melissa's other 'best friend'. Conversation continued in a desultory way as the three women moved around the room.

'How old is your little boy' the other friend asked Lee.

' The eldest is two, the other is just a baby.'

' I've got one of the terrible-twos as well. Aren't they

maddening at that stage of just saying 'No' to everything!'

Lee should have laughed and agreed but that only occurred to her later. Conscientiously truthful as always, she admitted 'Finn doesn't actually say 'no' very much. He's really helpful and co-operative... Er... I must be lucky.' Her voice, and the baby-chat, trailed away. Lee felt miserably let down that Melissa's other 'special' friend was so uninteresting – in fact, what she considered boringly straight. It seemed in some illogical but definite way personally threatening.

They left for home soon after midnight and, despite the superficial air of festivity, Lee felt a vague sense of menace postponed.

8

FESTIVITIES

A RIADNE ARRIVED next day rather later in the morning than was usual for her uninvited appearances. Lee was spreading washed, damp, baby clothes over the big fireguard to dry them off, Bruno was reading a sci-fi book and Elaine was looking through their paperbacks. Lee had bought some sticky-backed paper to make Christmas cards with Finn, who was solemnly sorting through the colours while he waited for her.

'I've just called to see if you'd like to come round tonight for supper,' said Ariadne, addressing herself to Lee as Bruno concentrated on his book.

'Oh, not tonight I'm afraid,' said Lee brightly, looking worriedly at Titty in case she was crumpling their coloured paper preparations in her snatching little hands. But Titty was looking very listless today. Her hair looked thinner than ever as it wisped out from under her pale bonnet and her eyes had bruise-dark rings under them. She stood by her mother, trembling a little, and made no move towards the toys today.

'I do wish you could,' sighed Ariadne, sounding more anxious than affected today. 'You could watch the Laugh-In – we've got BBC2, you know!'

Lee turned to Bruno, but he gave no help. She stooped to pick up the last of the baby clothes from the plastic bowl she was unloading, and Titty flinched and started to wail thinly.

'I'm sorry Ariadne, but not tonight. Perhaps some other night...' Ashamed of her excuse-less refusal and conscious of Bruno's continued heavy silence, she didn't offer Ariadne the usual cup of coffee and after a shorter lingering than usual,

Ariadne bundled herself off saying for about the third time 'Belfast is so boring, it doesn't seem like Christmas at all – I wish something nice was happening.'

Lee knew that the boredom Ariadne bemoaned could have been easily alleviated by any response from her. Almost any gesture or word would have made Ariadne an instant Cinderella, fantasising wildly and happily, her day transformed – and Lee knew how bleak these days could be.

'We could ask her to the party,' she complained tentatively to Bruno.

'Oh god no, Lee. You know what she's like.'

'They don't seem to be doing anything at all over Christmas or New Year – not even going to stay with family.'

'Not surprised. Who'd put up with them.'

After a while, still feeling guilty, Lee said 'Did you see Titty? Do you think she looked bruised?'

'I saw her when you moved her arm. She nearly took off.'

'Do you think she maybe gets thumped?'

'Looks like it.'

'Well maybe we should go round tonight – we might be able to help.'

'Lee stop kidding yourself. It's their lives, there's no help comes from interfering. And I'm not going round there again, once was enough. It's pigging and it's freezing and that husband of hers never shuts up – he's patronising and obnoxious, and she's an idiot.'

Elaine raised her eyebrows at the end of this emphatic tirade, but Lee answered snappishly 'They have no friends. Maybe they need help.'

'You can go and interfere if you like but you'll find it won't make a bit of difference – except to your ego.'

Lee sighed, more relieved than annoyed. The attack on her ego seemed to her entirely plausible and since she wasn't going anyway, it gave her a more acceptable reason not to intervene. It would just have been an ego-trip for me, she could reassure herself as she dismissed the idea of helping: it wouldn't have been any use for Titty or Ariadne, it would have just have been for me to feel I was being 'good'. This was a much more satisfactory reason.

'Hey, can I borrow this? It looks quite good,' said Elaine from the far end of the bookshelves.

'Yes, of course.' Lee answered without turning round.

'Can I have a bath at your place now?' Bruno asked Elaine as she got her things together to go, dropping the paperback copy of *Future Shock* into her bag. Lee and Bruno's bathroom was the coldest and most unsavoury room in the flat, so they used it as little as possible. The bath tap leaked, creating a constant frozen stalactite dangling over its murkily discoloured base, so Lee bathed the children in a big blue plastic wash-up bowl kept in the living room for that purpose and she and Bruno had developed the habit of using the least uncomfortable facilities of their friends. Lee went to Ian's because he lived the nearest, because his bathroom was warm and large, and because she was trying to make him feel more included in their group. It seemed to her that, because he was quite young for his role at the art college, he perhaps found it difficult to participate in their gatherings and this was why he had assumed a rather annoying role of superiority to screen his struggle. She had set herself to ease his path and so – although indebted to him for the undoubted favour of his hot water – Lee considered this a good exercise in social caring. Bruno usually went to Elaine's.

Elaine's place was impossible to take children, because everything was at floor level and so precariously placed it seemed it might be toppled by minor fluctuations of air current never mind the excited little fingers and indifferent little feet of children. From about three feet above floor level, all that happened on the bottle-green painted walls was Art Nouveau posters and a huge globular orange lampshade. Below that level, spread from wall to wall like a peacock's tail fanned for display, gaudily overlapped, were the emblems of Elaine's many magpie interests. Poetry books were heaped in piles, falling open at pages of Sylvia Plath or Stevie Smith, and Leonard Cohen LPs were propped against black lacquer pots and jugs. A frail plant survived somehow in a pot on a willow-patterned plate in the corner, surviving perhaps on black coffee absorbed from the atmosphere in lieu of water. Seating was supplied by floor cushions Elaine had created in leaf-green or cream satin. Most of the floor space, however, was covered with evidence of Elaine's chief passion, beyond even art or music or poetry, which was sewing. When Lee had last visited, she had been making herself a shirt – pale yellow with very full sleeves and a drooping collar. Scraps of primrose silk lay all around, as well as a pile of interesting-looking blue patterned satin. Lee's awe of any superior skill had full scope here: her own efforts to dress the children creatively seemed like dolls' clothes by comparison to Elaine's expertise, and her friend's flat seemed an exotic palace to her.

It was accepted that whoever went to Elaine's went alone, leaving the children with the other partner, and now as Bruno departed to ablute, Lee put Breff into his chair to watch while she helped his brother make christmas cards. Finn enjoyed the concept of licking the backs of the sticky coloured paper, and lapped at his pieces so avidly they became limp and the colour came off on his fingers, but on that day, none of that mattered. They were all quietly content. Lee stretched internally and luxuriated in the harmony of their domestic structure. It felt complete, and as close to perfect as a union could get. With herself and Bruno equal on the apex, their children could grow up secure and loved in spite of all the turmoil of Belfast around them. She wanted nothing more than the accepting connection they had in the fortress of friendship they'd built up around them. All those warm and loving remarks from their warm and loving friends seemed now to chime in her head to confirm this. In spite of this city, in spite of the conflict all around, they had found a peace and harmony, based on total sincerity, and on love.

Bruno was home rather later than Lee expected – not that it mattered, of course.

'Sorry I've been so long,' he explained immediately, 'I was trying on my new shirt! Elaine is making me one for Christmas.'

Lee was delighted and jealous in the same instant.

'How lovely! What's it like?'

'Oh it's grand. She's just got to finish it off, she'll be bringing it round over Christmas. Or, I might go and collect it before – if that's ok with you, Lee?'

On Christmas Eve Lee and Bruno embellished the entire flat ready for the festivities. They had a mass of decorations they had accidentally stolen from Guy the year before, when Tim and Siobhan had shared Christmas with them and arrived with boxes of streamers and tinsel and coloured balls all provided by the people who lived above Guy and had a key to his garage. 'Look!' they crowed, 'Guy's declaring his stationary business bankrupt and all this stuff is useless stock!'

'Great' said Bruno, and he and Lee promptly made another expedition there themselves to fetch further supplies. Several months later they found out that Guy's imminent bankruptcy was a false rumour, and it seemed too late then to give it all back, so when Tim and Siobhan moved on they had shared the booty conscientiously, and this year every inch of the living room was once again decked in tinselled glory. In the afternoon they went round to Sophia's flat and drank quite a lot of sherry while the children played.

Sophia was several years older than Lee, who perceived her as a clever woman wielding her sophistication with razor-sharp precision, and sometimes found her brittle elegance unnerving. Lee suspected that Sophia invited her and Bruno specifically to display her classless tolerance, as there was never anyone else there from their usual social circles. This afternoon Sophia's lover Frank was present, and also a woman called Rosalie who told Lee she had had all her Christmas food in the deep-freeze since September. Lee had only met one other person with a deep-freeze in her life so she expressed the respect that seemed due, although she felt rather sorry for Rosalie for missing out on all the fun of preparing for Christmas. Frank was an engineering lecturer, and while Lee appreciated his probing analytic mind probably made him excellent in his field, Lee felt it didn't make for easy conversation.

'Are you with anyone here?' was his opening, and when she identified Bruno, he was avid to probe further. Anything to do with Brian Boru, the 11th Century Irish King? Not from Brian? Was he German? Was he a dog, ha! ha! ha! No, seriously, Bruno (he said) 'is a strange name for an Irishman.' He made two words of his last one, as though 'Irish' were an adjective that qualified 'man', and not to his advantage. Lee bridled inwardly. 'Yes, isn't it,' she gushed, 'The pastor at his christening got confused, he was supposed to have been called Brutus – you know, like in Julius Caesar?' She had no intention of confiding that this ursine nickname was hers, inspired by his hirsute arms, and it had had caught on only because her husband clearly in no way suited his baptismal name of Gordon. Frank was now looking dubious so Lee added wildly 'Et Tu Brute! His parents were great lovers of Shakespeare.'

At this point Sophia removed her to meet some of the other guests. There were a few more lecturers from the College, including the Civil Rights campaigning tutor who Lee had already met in the pub. He was showing around the flyers of photographs of police beating up civilians. 'These are the ones they wouldn't let us publish,' he was saying, 'here you are, take this one – you'll get get done for illegal possession alright with that on you!'

Lee knew some of the students in the group he was addressing, including Sammy, known as 'the Stash' for his illegal pot plants and renowned for his belief in hash as the path to a truer consciousness.

'Did you get our card?' she asked him, with an innocent

smile, guessing he would rise to this opportunity to deplore the custom. The children had now participated in creating enough festive greeting cards from pictures and glue for Lee to distribute them around to almost everyone they knew.

Sammy obliged with a scoffing smile. 'Oh yes, thank you. You don't mind if we don't send one back do you? We're not conventional, as you know. Anyway Christmas is a really just a pagan festival.'

'I know, I'm a pagan. You can send us a dollop of brown rice, if you like, instead.'

'You don't understand the Eastern philosophy, Lee, or you wouldn't say things like that. They have tremendous acceptance of things we find difficult. They accept hunger, for instance.'

'They have to. Us Western philosophers don't allow them enough food because we take all their resources.'

'They could eat if they wanted to. Meat walks through their streets, but they won't touch it. The sacred cow represents an understanding that there is something more important than food. Man does not need to prey on other species.'

Lee thought about throwing in a question about how the inequalities of the caste system fitted with this idyll, but decided to pursue the diet theme.

'Why don't you try that, Sammy? A couple of spuds would be the Irish equivalent. But you like your meat and two veg! And nothing wrong with that – in a country with lots of both.'

'What's your point, Lee?'

'My point is that is that it's Marie who cooks it, every time. And she's the one who gave up her course when she fell pregnant. For all your oriental philosophies, you're just like your any old fella leaving the missus at home and going off on a Sunday morning. Only instead of the pub, you head for the hills to smoke hash and get stoned. And Marie's waiting at home, cooking your meal and looking after the wain. It doesn't really make any difference to her whether you're at the boozer or on a hillside in Lurgan – it's the traditional Irishwoman's role just the same.'

Lee had not meant to be so outspoken. She had kept her tone light and smiled at him throughout, so Sammy had the option to treat this tirade as mere jocularity, and he did so. He was not disturbed anyway, as he didn't consider the views of a housewife as likely to have much substance for reflection.

Lee turned to the buffet. Sophia always did things like that superbly, and she this party was no exception. The woman called Rosalie was at the far side of the room telling Marie that she had had all her christmas food in the deep freeze since September.

'God, Frank's wife is a drag,' muttered Sophia to Lee between the lips of her bright red smile. She stood pushing the cuticles of her immaculately maroon nails with the thumb of her other hand, gazing at her lavish costume rings. Sophia was wearing a magnolia coloured wool minidress and her long black hair was looped into an Edwardian bun that contrasted startlingly with her sharp, modern, face. The dress revealed her long slender legs but looked strangely juvenile for her sophisticated persona. Lee was wearing a deep purple dress in the now-more-fashionable length, but she felt gauche beside Sophia's self-assurance.

'Does Frank's... wife... know about you and him?'

Sophia shrugged elegantly. 'I don't really know. I suppose so.'

'Doesn't he tell her?'

'I shouldn't think he sits down and discusses his infidelities with his wife, would you?' said Sophia crisply. She clearly found Lee's naive curiosity amusing. Lee found her notion of sophistication barbaric.

Frank approached the buffet table and smiled at the two women who regarded him from deep within their own thoughts.

'This cheese is delicious,' he exclaimed, carving himself another chunk,'-what are the bits in it, caraway seed?'

'Salami' said Sophia glassily.

'Good God' said Frank, stopping abruptly mid-bite, 'Why didn't you tell me? You know I'm vegetarian.'

Sophia shrugged, registering neither grief nor satisfaction, and Lee was left marvelling at their social *sang-froid*, and bursting to laugh.

This was only an afternoon party, and well-timed sounds of strife from the upstairs room where all the children had been relegated gave the guests their cue for departure. Lee had plenty to say to Bruno on the way home.

'I think Sammy is terrible the way he leaves Marie at home and prides himself on being some kind of inspirational guru. After all, she was a student too until last year – she's had to give up everything. It's the old story, and he doesn't even recognise it. He thinks a weekly hash binge means he's liberated and progressive.' Lee did not smoke herself, regarding it as like gin, an expensive way to get stoned when wine was available. Bruno made thoughtful, tending-to-agree, kinds of sounds. He had occasionally joined Sammy in his sessions.

'I think the way we do things, sharing all the jobs, is much fairer,' Lee continued, 'and by the way, did you know that Frank was married to Rosalie?'

'Ah, yeah, I think I did.'

'I was a bit shocked that Sophia invited her actually. It's weird how she and Frank can keep up the pretence in public, acting like they hardly know each other and her calmly swapping recipes with his wife.'

'People are different,' suggested Bruno.

That evening Bruno went round to Elaine's for a short while while Lee finished making the waistcoats for the children and baked a batch of mince pies which didn't survive till the next day – indeed, they didn't survive very long after they were cool enough to touch.

On Christmas morning Lee woke to the delighted awareness that Breff had slept through his early morning feed, and the elation generated by this unexpected event carried her idyllically through the entire morning. All their small, secret, celebrations worked amazingly well too. Although they'd both agreed that, to save money, their gifts to each other would be just a bar of chocolate, (Fry's, which at fivepence was a penny less than Cadbury's), each surprised the other with a secret present on waking -- an extra half-bottle of whiskey for Bruno, and for Lee a copy not only of the latest *Sunday Times Magazine* but the *Radio Times Double Issue* too.

'Now you can choose all the stuff you want to watch with the boys, and cut up the pictures in the mags for your collages,' he explained, with the smugness of a mind-reader whose lucky guess has proved right, as she hugged him with squeals of delight.

'That must've cost you the best of four shillings!' Lee marvelled, and then 'Where's the paper parts, with the news and the sport and stuff?'

'Ah, I took that round to Elaine's – it would spoil the surprise if you'd seen that.'

'Well, there's loads of stuff to work with here,' Lee declared, 'fashions and music and adverts – ooh look, Twiggy's going to make a movie!'

She was happy to stay in bed browsing her treasure with the boys beside her, Finn investigating their stockings while Breff watched, till Bruno announced 'I'm going to make us all Christmas breakfast now!'

'Ooh, champagne and croissants? Kedgeree? Kippers?'

'Nah, porridge. We'd better get ourselves up, anyway, Elaine will be here soon -she's calling on her way to see a movie at QFT.'

'Is Queens Film Theatre open on Christmas day?' Lee wondered, as she began the nappy-changing process. Bruno said he didn't really know but Elaine clearly thought it was, and he went down to put the kettle on. Getting up was always as speedy a process as possible, to enable them to get down to the electric fire where the boys would be cursorily cleaned and dressed in whatever was warm and not too grubby. This morning Elaine arrived in time to ensure the boys could wear her presents for them – cosy jerkins as well as colourful tee-shirts and little denim jeans. For Bruno there was the promised shirt, in blue satin, and for Lee, a replica Laura Ashley party dress: flimsy white cotton, inset with panels of white *broderie anglaise*, threaded with slender white satin ribbons and tiny grey faux-pearl buttons. 'O god, this is gorgeous' Lee had groaned, then hugged Elaine tightly. 'It's like the wedding dress I never had! I love it so much.'

Elaine stayed for a post-breakfast sherry, sipped wandering round the room looking at all the greetings cards looped around the walls and criss-crossing the room on tinsel strings. 'You have so many friends!' she exclaimed as she paused at one large one, a glittering snow-scene. ('O god, that one from Ariadne looks ever so expensive, I only gave her a home-made one!' Lee sighed – 'You gave everyone home-made ones,' Bruno pointed out reasonably.) Elaine left them with promises to return next day to join them for a walk.

Miraculously, Christmas was being all that they wanted, and as the hours passed, Lee kept thinking wonderingly of the anti-climax that Christmas used to be when she was young, and feeling astounded by the good feeling of this one. Finn and Breff both seemed delighted with their 'main' present – a multi-storey car-park, with ramps the right width for their Matchbox cars, created out of pieces of wood by Bruno and decorated from sample paint pots by Lee – ("That's to be shared, now!" instructed their father) – and settled down to play together without any squabbling. The TV flickered in the corner most of the morning, churning out cartoons and comedy in a vague background of monochromatic benevolence until 'The Queen' at three alerted Bruno to the need for a break. 'We can put it on for the Disney classics later', Lee suggested, studying her listing-guide gift, but the boys seemed perfectly happy without the black and white flickering images in the corner. The day continued in a happy haze for Lee. She and Bruno sipped sherry most of the day, sharing sausages and crisps with the children for lunch. Paul and Cara dropped in briefly, but as Paul was tired and working that night, they didn't stay long. Josh and Rowena called round in the afternoon and joined in the drinking. Rowena was already plastered.

'Oh Lee, I must tell you,' she confided before they departed for a ritual Christmas tea at her mother's, 'Josh says he wants us to have two little boys exactly like yours – he says he wants our marriage to be exactly like yours – and so do I, so do I!' As Lee, somewhat overwhelmed, returned her weeping embrace, it seemed a valid ambition. Everybody should be lucky like this, should live and love like us, she felt, with no premonitory qualm at that supreme moment, on that Christmas day.

After the children were in bed and all the visitors had gone, Lee and Bruno ate their chicken dinner and slumped by the fire with a second bottle of wine to stare without much attention at the spangled banality of *Christmas Night With The Stars*. Melissa arrived halfway through the evening, with a tin of excruciatingly sickly home-made fudge in one hand and a steaming saucepan of fruit-laden punch in the other. 'I shall be sick if I consume another mouthful' promised Lee, eyeing a particularly malevolent-looking cherry with considerable unease. Melissa, undeterred, left the punch simmering in the kitchen until she had won them round to participation.

At about ten o'clock Tim and Siobhan called on their return from their day visit to Siobhan's mother, tense with hysterical mirth from several alcoholic family arguments and with a half-full bottle of whiskey that Tim's mother had surprised them by donating in recognition of the season of goodwill.

On Boxing Day Lee felt extremely frail and Bruno looked after the children, helped by Elaine. Ariadne attempted a visit, but he dealt with her efficiently and she did not stay.

And then Christmas was officially over. People still called in, and Bruno and Lee made visits too, but there seemed to be a sort of lull now, as if everything was building up almost consciously to the next climax: the New Year's Eve party at Lee and Bruno's.

9

NEW YEAR 1971

NEW YEAR'S EVE dawned freezing and began for Lee just before six when the shivering figure of Finn appeared in the doorway of their bedroom, crying with cold. Against their usual policy, Lee pulled him into bed with them to cuddle. She was amazed that the winter could get any colder, but consoled herself against the bitter morning with the prospect of the evening ahead. Cara called in the afternoon to offer help with preparations, but since these consisted merely in accumulating any available drinking receptacle, retrieving the wax-dripped wine bottles from their box in the back-yard to act as candle-holders, and putting out sticks of french bread and chunks of cheddar cheese, Lee declined gratefully.

People began arriving early. Tim and Siobhan were as usual among the first, this time with brandy. Lee drank a tumbler-full on top of several mugs of wine, and the evening dissolved into a happy haze. She remembered kissing several people and dancing almost constantly for hours. She remembered seeing Bruno and Elaine in a close embrace, and noticed that Ian Kingston, followed her gaze and then moved towards them apparently reprovingly. How odd, she thought, does he think I mind Bruno and Elaine kissing? She also remembered, clearly, dancing with Paul in the centre of the hot and hectic room, dancing a slow dance within his arms, at first reluctant because she preferred the fast dances, then slowly aware of a mutually intense consciousness of their connection that became almost mesmeric as Paul crouched his tall body over her, a consciousness that seemed primal, and then so raw and naked that Lee stared amazed into his intent eyes. Paul, Paul, she whispered. And Paul whispered back, I know, I know, with an enigmatic intensity that left Lee quivering.

After that dance she left the room, pulled someone's coat from the heap on the stairs, and ran down the road to the phone box, where she called a friend in England. 'Mikki I love you, I really do,' she solemnly told her friend, another young mother who she exchanged long letters with every week but had not seen since the time they shared a flat together before her marriage. 'That's nice,' replied the pleased and sleepy voice of Mikki, several hundred miles away. Lee remembered all this, clearly and regretlessly, in the cold sobriety of the first day of the 1971.

That day Guy came round with a bottle of wine as an apology for his unnoticed absence the night before. They drank it in the evening. Lee looked at old photographs and Bruno worked out some song chords with a merchant seaman called Sam who had arrived at the party the night before with a mandolin and introduced himself as a folk enthusiast, and stayed on.

'I wish I could paper a room with blow-ups of all these people,' said Lee, looking at the photographs of all the faces of college friends she was unlikely to smile at again, 'It's so sad the way people move away from you, and nothing survives.'

'It's better like that,' said Bruno, bent over the machine heads he was tuning to get his guitar in key with the mandolin. 'We can all get on with our lives.'

'I suppose so.' said Lee. She wished Paul and Cara would come round, wanting coffee and gossip about last night, making everything normal, so she could resolve some of the tension that seemed to linger like a kind of backwash from that strange drunken encounter during the dancing. But they didn't call that evening and Lee, exhausted and tense with anticlimax, went to bed early. She lay listening to Bruno and Sam playing and singing downstairs. Next day she still felt restless and unmollified.

'We must get a sitter tonight, I simply must get out.' It was two days later, and Lee stood in the living room staring, panicky with aversion, at surroundings that had morphed somehow from magical to unbearable. The paraphernalia of Christmas that earlier had cast a glitzy spell now looked tawdry as cards hung slewed at angles on dribbles of coloured crepe and the tired tree seemed overwhelmed by its gaudy load. The whole room now seemed top-heavy with glitter and banality.

'It's just anti-climax, after the last few days being so full-on,' she told the faded curtains, yearning through them to the dark street. A couple came out of the cafe opposite and the automatic doors swung slowly shut. Lee watched while the couple seemed poised in indecision, or perhaps dispute, before walking slowly up the street together. It seemed to be still raining.

Lee was conscious of an irrational frenzy of impatience and an increasing conviction she couldn't tolerate remaining caged in this room all evening. 'It's just anti-climax' she whispered again to herself, struggling to rationalise this inability to relinquish the glamour of their festivities and accept the normal simplicity of a quiet evening at home.

'Can't we just go out for a bit?' she couldn't resist pleading.

'Well we can't get Paul or Cara,' said Bruno dubiously, 'Paul's working. I tell you what, James's on the phone. I'll nip down the road and give him a ring and see if he or Fionnula could come down. I can't think of anyone else – everyone's booked up tonight.'

Lee hesitated, reluctant because neither James nor Fionnula had ever offered to babysit, but her hunger to get out of the flat won her over. Bruno returned shortly from the phone box to say James and Fionnula had been settling down to a quiet evening's drinking but had agreed, with minimum reluctance evident, to shift their venue, and would be around shortly. Lee hurried to go and change.

The went to the Ploughman's Head. Bruno talked about

the possibilities of working the Belfast folk clubs with his new-found mandolin-playing friend.

'There might be a bit of money in it, too,' he said. Lee had been wanting to talk to him about her experience at the party, but it was all so strange she didn't know how to shape it into a coherent account. At ten o'clock when time was called, as they got up to go she said 'Would you go on trusting me, whatever I did, Bruno?'

He took her question seriously enough to consider it while he put on his jacket.

'I think so,' he finally answered.

'Even if you knew I had made love with someone else?' The question seemed strangely amicable.

'Put it this way, love' said Bruno, collecting his change and his fag packet from the table, 'I always behave as I want, and I assume you'll do the same.'

They left the pub.

Perhaps the elation of possibility, the totally-surprising, though totally-predictable, sanction suddenly given like an extra christmas present, was still fizzing in her head when Lee got back. Perhaps the start of the drama had already begun at the flat, planted by her feverish discontent earlier that evening. Perhaps James and Fionnula had been talking in the same way too. Perhaps all their awarenesses fused at the moment when Bruno and Lee re-entered their flat, now no longer hostile to her but welcoming, and perhaps there was a trail of inevitability about everything that followed although at the time it had all seemed to Lee so unexpected and extraordinary.

James and Fionnula seemed to have drunk more during their babysitting stint than the other couple had consumed at the pub. The red-dimmed lighting and record player were still set up from the party, and the room was still cleared as if for dancing. A *Cream* album, not yet reclaimed, was playing and Bruno started immediately dancing with Fionnula, so Lee and James danced together too. Afterwards Lee wasn't quite sure of the sequence of events, how at some point the two couples had become separated, why her husband and her dance partner's wife seemed to be in another room. Lee, engrossed as always in the movement of the dance, was becoming aware of the effects of the extra alcohol which was making her feel as if she was flowing into the sound, and the room seemed thick with anticipation. James's face, grinning from the drink and the dancing, seemed the centre of this. Then James wasn't dancing with her any more and Fionnula was talking to her in the strangest way. Fionnula must be very drunk. Fionnula seemed to be pleading with her about something. 'Don't do it,' Fionnula was saying. Lee was aghast and instantly inquisitive, and Fionnula went on. 'You could do it. You're so sexy. You're so sexy.'

Lee was enflamed with the possibilities of this astounding accolade, and greedily absorbed the pleading flattery as if it were a mystic code, without engaging with either the reason or the meaning. The atmosphere was dynamic, incoherent yet urgent, as Fionnula lit the fuse. Her final words compounded the confusion of emotions now burning in Lee's befuddled mind:

'If I could go with anyone else except James,' she said, 'It would be Bruno.'

And then she seemed to fade, like a sprite in a Shakespearian fantasy whose role is to bewilder the bewitched protagonists into some path of folly or tragedy that will act itself out inevitably in time.

The interlude had a weird effect on Lee. Her normal response to unexpected data was immediate and intense analysis, but that night her greedy confusion had only one awed response – a physical one. James? He fancied Cara, everyone knew that, and Cara carried that knowledge proudly like a medal from old campaigning days. James found Lee sexy? Fionnula's extraordinary message had somehow not registered as the prohibition of her pleading words, it seemed instead an initiation to a secret strata of their friends' lives. Proximity and private thrill worked their own logic, and when James returned to continue the dance it was as though a silent signal had passed between them.

He changed the LP, and grabbed her again to dance. They were alone now in the living room and the dance was becoming an enclosing framework for the pattern of actions that must now begin. *What a drag it is getting old*, wailed the Stones, as Lee and James moved rhythmically towards each other and apart. Lee was conscious she was staring at James now, and his eyes held her locked as the dance moved on and the taut void closed inevitably.

The record stopped. Another clipped down to replace it. This was a fast tempo, really fast, and Lee accelerated with quick little jump-taps to meet the rhythm. But James stopped dancing and stared at her.

'We'll go and get some more drink from my place,' said James, and they called out as they left that this was their intention.

'Is that alright?' Lee begged Bruno from the door.

'I'll be here with the kids', he said. Fionnula was not visible and, after her previous suggestive words, Lee felt she must already be upstairs.

James drove Lee to his flat, which to Lee's awe had central heating. He was one of the few in their crowd with a job and their flat was modern but it still felt like a sci-fi luxury to have a radiator. He poured them both brandies from a bottle on a tray of drinks on the sideboard – another surreal luxury – and then said 'Let me show you my mother's wedding present to me,' as he pulled his wallet from his back pocket. The present was a letter, folded into creases that were already nearly rips, and in the dim light of the red-shaded lamp, Lee read 'This is to notify you that I no longer have a son. Do not contact me again.' It was signed with a surname – his surname – and the prefix 'Mrs'.

It took Lee a few moments to assimilate what she had seen. Rows, yes. A beating even. But to be disowned by your mother, for loving the wrong girl? To receive a message like that, like a formal warning, like an angry threat to an importunate stranger, a notification of unforgivable transgression... Lee realised she had whimpered aloud on sight of the words and didn't know what else to say so she said nothing. James had seen her eyes spilling, that was probably enough.

He refolded the letter and put it back in his wallet. Then he slung his jacket on the floor and lifted her from the settee and began to pull off her dress. His urgency was making him clumsy so Lee took over and left him to disrobe himself and pull out the sofabed. It didn't take long: they were soon back at Bruno and Lee's flat, where they found Bruno alone. Fionnula had disappeared.

The rest of the night – it was now nearly 3 a.m. – passed in a strangely calm manner. Lee was split between guilty responsibility, or rather irresponsibility, and puzzled indignation. They conferred, sobered and anxious: Bruno had dozed and then woken, he said, and was now clearly confused as well as concerned. James seemed incapable of any decision.

'She'll have gone to Cara's,' Lee said, suddenly inspired.

'D'you think so?' Bruno sounded baffled, and she felt suddenly strong, and certain that she could fix this mess.

'Cara was on her mind earlier tonight, and she wouldn't have tried to walk all the way back to your place, would she?'

'I suppose not,' James mumbled. He looked at her hopefully.

'I'll go down to Cara's,' Lee said, 'and see if she's there.'

For some reason not clear to herself she wanted Cara to know about the events of the evening, although whether in hope of finding Fionnula safe or some less innocent reason she did not, at that time, query. It was logical, though, as they hadn't passed Fionnula on their drive back, which would surely have been likely.

'Worth a try, ' Bruno said to James, and James shrugged in a 'Guess so' sort-of way, and Lee shivered her way hurriedly down the short road that divided their two homes.

Cara was in, alone, and still awake. She provided coffee and listened attentively. Lee reflected later that the reception a wakeful person gives to an incoherent story of fornication and flight at 2 o'clock in the morning is probably different from that of a just-roused person, because Cara was instantly and avidly alert.

'She's not been here,' she said, 'I'd have heard the bell. I never sleep sound while Steve's on his shift, I can't settle. So – what were you guys up to? How was it supposed to work?'

Cara was so factual in her curiosity that it somehow seemed quite natural to relate the evening's bizarre events. She kept it brief.

'I was having a real bad evening, anti-climax now all the parties are over, so they came over to sit while me and Bruno went out to the pub. When we got back, they suggested the swap thing, and we did it, using both our houses, but now Fionnula's run off and we don't know where she's gone.' She didn't mention James's terrible memento of lost mothering, though in some ways this still seemed the most important part of the story.

'She'll be at home,' Carla suggested, with a surprising amount of certainty.

'Let's hope. Anyway, I can't stay because they're waiting for news.' Calmed though still bewildered, Lee hurried back up the road to the waiting men.

'We'd better go out and look for her in your car,' said Bruno, and James silently followed him out.

Lee cleared up and for the second time that night undressed, and settled herself in a bed, trying not to think. Her mind kept returning to the letter that James had shown her. She tried to pity the woman who had lost her son but she could not. For some reason she kept losing track of the word 'disowned' as if were simply too painful to hold in her head. Displaced, she thought, groping towards the right term, and then, we are all displaced people here.

Lee realised she wanted a coffee but she couldn't face the cold of the kitchen. She turned on the tranny, and re-tuned to an early morning talk programme. Somebody was being interviewed about their concern over the rubber bullets now being used by soldiers. 'They're not properly tested', the voice was saying, 'do the soldiers not realise they can cause serious injuries? Firing low is not an answer – they'll take a child's eye out some day.' Lee twiddled the setting back to music.

Next day she took both Finn and Breff into bed and they all had breakfast together huddled in blankets. It was still cold. Eventually Lee left Bruno to a further lie-in and, wrapping the children as warmly as possible, set off to confirm to Cara that all was now well: Bruno had arrived after his long walk back from James's house to report, with no particular emotion other than tiredness, that Fionnula had made it home.

She met Paul on her way down and they fell in step and walked down the road together. Breff was in the pushchair and his brother alternately trailed behind and darted ahead, as they walked quietly along the dreary terraced street. It was bin day, and dustbins dragged from their yards lurked sullenly at the kerb edge waiting to be emptied. Lee frequently had to call out to Finn not to touch the rubbish which he kept reaching curiously towards.

'Cara told me about last night,' Paul said, half hesitant, half confidential, after some desultory conversation, and Lee met his eyes briefly searching for interpretation but he looked quickly away.

'Oh, yes,' said Lee, 'It was a bit of a strange scene.' How odd, she thought, our silent conversation is. He's saying, Cara told me that you and a friend of mine threshed together at his flat last night. I wonder if he thinks, two nights ago that lovemaking could have been with me. I wonder if he knows how I wanted it to be.

Melissa was at the flat when she got back, Lee was pleased to see. Melissa's blatant fondness for Bruno would, she thought, be a reassurance if he was feeling bad about the strange end to their enterprise the previous night. She settled the children with toys and and confided the tale as soon as Bruno had left for his afternoon session at the library.

'Do you feel bad about it?' asked Melissa.

'A bit,' Lee admitted.

'Because of Fionnula?'

'Not really because of Fionnula – that was James's responsibility, I suppose, to realise that she wasn't happy even though she seemed keen. I mean, I'm really sorry if Fionnula felt upset but people can't own other people, can they? Even if they've got a certificate. I don't mean, 'Let do what thou wilt be the whole of the law' like Aleister Crowley, obviously, but I do think 'Make Love Not War' is a useful guideline.'

'So… what's the problem?' Melissa seemed dissatisfied with Lee's disclaimer and Lee remembered now that she had set her hopes on Bruno.

'It's a cultural thing, I guess. People here think they understand free love, but they don't. They want it like magic stardust, but if it's in real life then it's going be difficult sometimes, like everything is. And especially for Ulstermen, their outlook is so dogmatic and judgemental. James will think less of me now, it's his upbringing. And… Paul will too.'

'Nonsense, Lee – everybody loves you!' Melissa was parodying her own warmth in a way Lee knew was intended to comfort her. So Lee shrugged and laughed, but underneath, despite her analysis, she did feel hopeful. Nobody gets away with anything, she had always insisted, but within her a tiny voice whispered, but perhaps you will.

'Stay for tea, Melissa. I got my family allowance out today, and we've spent it all on booze and Bruno phoned Tim and Siobhan, they're coming round.'

'Well I'll stay for the booze, but I won't eat a thing,' said

Melissa, and hurried down to the off-licence for 'plonk' to add to the shared pool. Half way through the evening Paul and Cara appeared too, brandishing an impulse-bought bottle of Bacardi.

'We haven't got a sitter' exclaimed Cara, guiltily triumphant at truanting from her responsibilities, 'We just thought, to hell with it – let's go for a jar, and then at ten we didn't feel like going home, so we're here!'

'The wee shite is probably yelling her head off,' supplemented Paul, laughing.

Tim, who had borrowed Siobhan's brother's car for the night, noted Lee's alarmed face and said quickly 'I'll take a run down in the car and look at her for you.'

'Nah, let her yell.' said Paul cheerily and then, quickly, 'No, seriously, she never wakes in the evening, she'll be alright.'

It wasn't really a party. They had been talking about the tarring and feathering, but once Paul and Cara arrived the serious conversation morphed into banter. Lee felt again the undercurrent of their strange recent intimacy and as her favourite Peter Sarstedt album was playing it seemed quite natural that she and Paul should start dancing. Tim and Siobhan were dancing too, and when Bruno and Cara disappeared into the kitchen to make coffee Melissa announced herself exhausted and left. Tim and Siobhan went down to the car to fetch some whiskey to go with the coffee.

Then an extraordinary thing happened. At least it seemed extraordinary to Lee, who was perhaps allowing herself to be deceived by the simplicity of these particular moves. Bruno and Cara came back from the kitchen and Cara said cheerfully 'We've decided that two of us can go down to our place and two of us can stay here. Any preference? Samantha will probably howl in the morning.'

Paul said he was easy and they all looked enquiringly at Lee who immediately said 'go'. She wanted to leave straight away, like a child promised a picnic, and the others told her to wait until Tim and Siobhan had gone home. 'Why? Why not now?' she remembered afterwards urging, as though it were not something dangerous they all were holding between them, a bomb that threatened the universe as she had known it. After the mess and confusion of unclear decisions, this simple plan couldn't possibly go wrong.

So after Tim and Siobhan had left, Lee and Paul hurried down the mealymouthed little street to the house where he lived with Cara. The child had apparently not woken as she lay serene on the mattress in the corner of her room, which was kept fully darkened by the closed door.

Lee found Paul and Cara's unfamiliar bedroom exciting. There were discarded clothes and boxes of stuff, and the candy-strip sheets were wrinkled and slightly grubby. They undressed and Paul got on the bed.

'Are you nervous?' he asked.

'Not really' said Lee, after considering for a moment.

'I am,' said Paul and he lifted her on top of him.

Why what followed was so incredible Lee never fully understood. They seemed ready for each other in an extraordinary way, careful and intent, like quiet explorers tracking the source of some elemental necessity. Once, when she was on top of him and he held her up by her armpits like a child and they stared at each other, Paul said 'I love you Lee, is that wrong?' and she had whispered with a vehemence she had fully believed 'No. Love is never wrong.' It had seemed then the most utterly beautiful of all tautologies in a reality more real than anything else in her life. Later, as she recalled their words and remembered his lean body flushed and naked, it seemed strange that the universe had ever contained such an episode, and incredible that she had participated. Later, she recalled, coldly aghast at her arrogance, how it had really seemed that night as though they had grasped the key to some mighty hidden door of liberation which would now swing open, never to close again.

She did have one moment of doubt. Towards morning Paul said, 'It hasn't been so good for a long time.' In this place of beautiful redemption there should be no comparisons, Lee thought. I shan't think like that, she decided, and lay quiet in Paul's arms, throbbing with sweet and languid exhaustion.

In the morning, still light-headed, still exhilarated, they dressed the child and drank coffee as the little girl ate her porridge eyeing them curiously, and then all three set off back up the street to Lee and Bruno's flat. There was an early morning hazy fog and a milky sun filter through the chill air. Women in bedroom slippers and curlers darted across the street on inscrutable errands. Tiredly, Lee and Paul meandered up the street, hands mingling, the little girl singing contentedly to herself.

IO

AFTERMATH

B REAKFAST was still in progress at the flat when Lee and Paul arrived. Lee made more coffee, and the children were left to play together while the parents sat together relaxed, smiling at each other and yawning. It was Cara who suggested the pub. Everyone else quickly agreed, and equipped themselves and the children.

The local pub was nearly empty when they arrived, and the publican had no objection to the three children being settled on the narrow bench with crisps and squash to keep them contented. It was Paul who spotted the juke box.

'Hey, what about this? Anyone remember Frank Ifield?' Bruno produced a tanner and soon they were all joining the crooning chorus of his ten-years-old chart-topper: *'When they ask me to recall, the thrill of them all, I will tell them I remem... ber.... yoooo!'* They all ended on a different note, pointing at each other and the children too, then laughing and hugging each other.

I am so proud of us, thought Lee, we have done something fantastic, she thought. We have done something that's supposed to be furtive or tiredly decadent and we've made it marvellous. The triumph of love over convention. We've opened doors and left them wide, we've started something impossible, that's everything I ever wanted. Within the framework of our society, without rejecting its structures, we've claimed that it is possible to extend love, and shown that love need never involve pain. We have taken on the responsibility of loving one another without hurting, without resenting, without claiming or intruding. I'm confident we can do it.

She was wrong, of course. Nobody gets away with anything, she had acknowledged to Melissa, and then in the arrogance of bliss she had thought that the four of them could somehow override and rewrite the history of human experience. In the blurred confusion that followed, Lee remembered that scene at the pub clearly, remembered how they had all met each others' eyes smiling, and how she had burned with happiness and believed she would escape pain because she made no demands on the future. She had thought herself, then, able to accept whatever might follow, whether nights of love or not, in the closeness between all of them that she was sure would never falter now. She was not equipped for what actually happened after that first day, which was silent, undiscussed and unspeakable, retreat.

Paul did not at first obsess her mind. It was only when he had become unapproachable that she realised with dismay that the unrequited need to see and talk to him was not abating, but growing. Paul's image, sometimes vague and sometimes poignantly exact, began to obsess her, not as a need but as a loss: his remembered words were vivid but now incomprehensible.

That was all later. The first day was idyllic. They bought food on the way back from the pub: a tin of mince and some spaghetti and biscuits and milk. By unspoken agreement Cara and Lee made lunch for both families in the flat. In the evening they parted, but as though incapable of ever relinquishing closeness, they had been drawn together again once the children were in bed. Bruno took the remains of the beer down to Paul's while Cara came up to spend the evening with Lee.

Cara had bought a new dress for the next Saturday party, and brought it up to show Lee. 'I just thought I'd let you see,' she said conspiratorially as she undid her maxi-coat. The dress was white, in a kind of grecian style and Cara had pulled her hair partly on top of her head so it hung loose below. She looked to Lee like an Ingres painting. Lee caught her breath in admiration.

I shall never surpass this happiness, Lee thought, and that at least turned out to be right. This was just another of the irreconcilable recalled images in the maelstrom of emotion in the days that followed. Later, when Lee saw the dress at a party and noticed its glossy nylon texture, it seemed slightly sleazy.

As January dragged by, Paul withdrew completely although she still saw Cara almost daily. Cara seemed in good form. She talked to Lee with unabated friendliness, never mentioning the swap, ignoring that night as if it had never happened, and Lee was afraid to speak of it now. Between herself and Bruno an indefinable barrier seemed to have come down: for the first time, lying beside Bruno at night, Lee found she could not talk of her experiences or analyse her feelings. She missed this achingly. She and Bruno lay silent now after love-making, and Lee wondered if he too was wondering what comparisons were being fought off in the miserable darkness of the night.

In her initial confusion Lee first turned to Melissa. She would have preferred to lick her wound in silence, but her unrequited longing for analysis and interpretation demanded some salve. It would, she thought, be helpful to put ordinary words to the trauma of loss.

'It's the broken connection, you see,' she explained, 'I don't know if Paul regrets everything so much he's ashamed, or if he's afraid I'll try to make an ongoing thing of it . Or if it's something else – but whatever his reason, we could surely still talk to each other – we've been friends for years!'

Melissa held Lee's hand and looked sympathetic, but her eyes were sparkling.

'Wittgenstein!' she breathed, '"The limit of my language is the limit of my world." What a marvellous example! I've just been exploring a digression on exactly that concept – that if we cannot think about something, we cannot talk about it – and both sides then become unthinkable. I've actually got the book here!'

'Ah, so you have,' said Lee dully, as Melissa pulled from her bag a small hardback entitled *Tractatus Logico-Philosophicus.* 'Is there anything in there about how to deal with it? I mean, psychologically?' She resisted adding, Since you are, after all, supposed to be on a psychology research project not a literary quiz. This was not going the way she had hoped.

'We could both drop in on Cara this evening, while Paul's at work, and I'll appraise the context?' Melissa suggested.

Lee felt uncomfortable about this suggestion and also, now, about their conversation. Spying and gossiping was not what she had in mind. She suspected Melissa wanted to see if the ending of their foursome meant Bruno was available, and began to regret telling her anything. Is this what will happen now, she wondered, no more honesty in any of our friendships?

'Actually I think I'd be better taking an early night tonight,' she said, adding miserably 'Can we let it all drop now? We can talk later, when I've got something more to say.'

That week Lee developed a throat infection that made speech difficult, and eating impossible. Looking after the children became a struggle, but Bruno was busy all day now term had restarted and in the evenings he went over to Sam's digs to practise in their newly-formed duo. Lee spent her evenings alone once the children were in bed, staring at the TV with the sound turned up just loud enough to muffle the street sounds, these days a regular nightly reminder of the hostilities mounting outside. The late night radio news marked her evenings in terms of growing menace. 'There were riots tonight in the Ballymurphy area of Belfast...' the neutral voice of the reporter intoned. 'Rioting broke out in the Ardoyne area of Belfast...' 'Today, riots in the Shankhill Road area of Belfast...'

This was how Paul found her the first time he returned to the flat since that evening. Lee was hunched up in her old sweater on top of Bruno's pyjamas, hugging her knees and staring at her little ice-white toes, which however much they wriggled seemed unable to warm up. She felt dreadfully sorry for them. It wasn't their fault, any of this, and now they were suffering the misery of the rest of her. There was a sound of someone coming upstairs – the back door must have been left unlocked. Lee was aware of the door pushed open behind her and with immense effort turned her head. Paul. He hesitated in the doorway.

'Bruno said you were sick. I'm sorry.'

Lee with great effort inclined her head in assent, and spoke thickly.

'Do you want coffee?'

'No, I can't stop. I'm on my way to work.'

He hesitated, as if pity was making him uneasy. Lee thought how abject and dreadful she must look with her straggled greasy hair, sick swollen face, and tears of self-pity brimming intractably behind her lashes. She avoided his gaze, making her breathing shallow and inaudible to try to minimise the sound of her shivering. She turned her head away and did not look back when he said 'Well, I'd better be getting along,' but nodded and sat listening for the door closing behind him.

Some time after his receding footsteps had been replaced by silence Lee found to her surprise she still had not started crying. The pain behind her eyes seemed too intense now for any such relief, so she remained dry-eyed staring at the TV and listening for the half-obliterated shouts in the streets outside.

By the next weekend Lee had recovered enough to go with Bruno and Melissa to a Psychology Department party at the flat of one of the lecturers. She decided this would be a fresh start for her – a chance to put her difficult start to the year into proportion as just that – not a life-changer, just a … difficult start. The crowd would be mostly unknown to her, and she could present herself against a new backdrop. Some kind of onward movement was not just welcome, but essential. Lee chose her outfit carefully: wraparound skirt, russet with golden threads, low-cut black top, gipsy earrings. Warmest coat and thick boots, but she'd take them off when she got there – it would be warm enough.

It was a fairly small party and everyone seemed to know one another quite well. Melissa introduced her to two men, a beautiful student who looked like a Renaissance painting of Jesus, whose name Lee didn't hear, and a lecturer, who Lee recognised vaguely as a friend of Sophia's. At Sophia's gathering he had looked like Pooh Bear at Glyndebourne and tonight he looked like Pooh Bear bemused by flower power. He immediately wanted to dance with her, and romped through a couple of rock numbers until a slow record came on and he surged in on her like Pooh Bear determined to scoop honey.

'Did you know you are rather sweet?' he murmured fruitily.

'Excuse me a moment,' said Lee, and she went into the dark bedroom and lay on the bed with the coats, staring at the unfamiliar outlines of furniture and breathing quietly in the gradually increasing gloom of the room.

Some time later the beautiful-Jesus student entered and contemplated her.

'What are you doing?'

Lee removed her thumb from her mouth.

'I'm being a coat.'

He contemplated the prospect.

'Can I be a coat, too?'

'Alright,' said Lee limply.

They lay side by side among their fabric counterparts, not touching, eyes level, staring darkly in the dimness. The lecturer came in looking for Lee. He switched on the light as he entered and then abruptly switched it off and left, shutting the door tight.

'It's very dark now,' said the student, after a while.

'Coats don't mind the dark,' Lee reminded him.

After a long pause he said 'I find I'm a scarf now.'

Lee giggled. She thought about being a scarf and then decided 'Coats are better.'

'They do offer more scope,' the voice in the darkness agreed.

Lee put her hand out and touched the long beautiful scarf beside her.

'I don't know you but I like everything about you,' the scarf told her softly and solemnly.

The coat rumpled across the bed and nestled against the scarf and they both lay quiet and protective against each other for a long while, until Melissa came in and found them and immediately went to fetch Bruno.

'Let's all go to your place,' she organised, and they complied.

He knelt before her caressing her as she stood, touching his hair. His is so very beautiful, Lee thought dispassionately. She surveyed his naked body with appreciation but no desire. She wished he would not kiss her there, as she'd only just finished a period and felt repulsed at the idea he might find her distasteful. Later, when she recalled their copulation, she felt no sensation except unimpaired affection, like a cripple promised faith-healing who does not blame the gentle caressing fingers because they cannot heal.

It was the following week. Lee trembled in the chair in the doctor's surgery. He wrote briefly on his pad and then turned genially to her.

'Well, Lee, how can I help you this time?'

'I wondered if you could give me anything to relax,' Lee mumbled, 'It's the baby – he keeps being sick and it's really getting to me.'

'When you say 'being sick', it this just this posseting we've discussed before?'

'Yes. I know you say it's nothing to worry about but he's constantly doing it now, and it's smelly and it gets on my nerves. I have to wash his sheets every day. And I get so exasperated

I'm afraid I may hurt him. When he screams I have to leave him alone – I daren't touch him in case I find myself hurting him. This morning' – tears started brimming and falling at the appalling recollection – 'I was trying not to touch him, not to hurt him, and I found myself spitting at him.'

The doctor told Lee there was no need for her, for either her or her baby, to suffer in this way. What he was prescribing, he explained, would relax her and disperse the feelings of hostility. There was no need for her to feel guilty, he said, writing quickly on his prescription pad. Lee could not hear all of what he said because several fire engines went past at that moment, but she took his piece of paper gratefully. 'I'm sorry, doctor,' she began, and then thought how boring it must be hearing apologies from neurotic patients, and she left.

It was later. Lee came back from shopping. Sam and Bruno, wreathed in cigarette smoke, were playing guitars.

'Bad news for you, love. I'm stopping for tea,' said Sam cheerfully.

Lee was pleased: this announcement usually meant a pound of sausages as a donation, which was always helpful. She went to the kitchen to investigate. There were sausages, a loaf, and some tomatoes. Bruno followed her down.

'Where's the cloth, love, there's been some coffee spilt.'

Lee passed it across.

'Paul was here earlier,' said Bruno as he took it.

Lee stared at the extra coffee cup left on the draining board. She pictured Paul sitting in the flat drinking from it, smoking and talking, and herself, subdued and harassed, entering and leaving shops, with clouded mind and groceries.

'How the hell am I supposed to integrate these with a casserole?' she demanded, poking at the sausages. The sight of them in their plastic wrapping caused a pain in her stomach.

Bruno looked surprised. 'You don't have to. Just fry them up, we'll have them extra.'

'Well I don't want any.'

'Well don't bloody have any.' Bruno banged the door on his way back to the living-room.

Lee threw the pack of sausages on the floor and after a moment's reflection pushed the bread and tomatoes after them. She contemplated dumping the casserole on top but something about that seemed too irrevocable so she collected up the stuff and put it back on the sideboard. She stood for a while picking at her arm abstractedly with the tip of the kitchen knife, trying to make it bleed along the tiny blue vein. Eventually, silently crying again, she went to fetch the pan and started to fry the sausages.

That week, they found out about Ariadne in what seemed the most horrible way, by chance, though perhaps all ways would have been equally horrible. What seemed the most absurd and dreadful part of all to Lee was that she had not even missed her. The dreary days had dragged by without her noticing how long it was since that familiar coy, coquettish, supplication 'It's only me!' had heralded Ariadne traipsing up the stairwell. Now that the plague from which they had prayed release had actually been lifted, they had not merely not cared – they had not even noticed. Perhaps after all Ariadne had not been so very dreadful. Perhaps she had even been necessary, to boost their egos at the low times, to reassure them by comparison how witty and intelligent they were. She was dead now, anyway, as they discovered by suddenly realising the implication of a casual conversation with an acquaintance who collected his dole on the same day as LeRoy, and had heard from others queuing that LeRoy had left town since his wife committed suicide. She had drowned herself in the Lagan, near their home. Apparently there had been a row – a child had been hurt – might have had to go to hospital or perhaps taken by social services – their informant didn't really know – and the wife had jumped off the Embankment into the black water and though there were people about, no-one had realised it till later. Or they thought it was another scuffle, or something. Anyway, everyone had kept away, and the father was gone now too so nobody really knew anything more.

Lee heard this tale several times as it became common currency. It was retold without malice but with the relish that people living close to chronic generalised grief and trauma inevitably bestow on a specific tragedy. In the drab frustration of their days this was a vivid cameo, and was treasured as such in the telling. Lee became hypersensitive to these now familiar conversations. The image of Ariadne's bloated body, bloated still more by the river whose glittering waters she had so recently extolled as pure and perfect, was too horrible to be contained in lament for Ariadne only: the horror seeped out and contaminated all those who obsessively retold it. Lee was increasingly appalled. Their fascination revolted her, and their indifference seemed to make them close to murdering her themselves. Perhaps she feared indifference was the real killer, and dared not contemplate the indifference that had preceded this death. Lee mourned in a dreadful dark secret way that she knew was, in part at least, a selfish grief for herself. Why had she so callously resisted the obvious truth of Ariadne's pleading, in those days when she herself had seemed to have so much? Lee had believed that she had enough warmth and love for the whole world, and that insouciant ill-founded confidence had dazzled poor Ariadne. It was all gone now, and she had never given Ariadne anything. Inside that gross and silly woman with the pleading tittering voice was someone real and drowning all those months: the river had only caught up with her. She was floundering in inner tears long before. All those contrived little attacks on Titty which Lee had thought half-concealed she now saw were half-public pleas for help. How could she have been so wilfully blind? Despair made all things clear. Now I know the broken road you trod, Lee prayed to the ghastly river-sodden Buddha in her mind who cried and cried with Ariadne's big spiky-lashed eyes, but the penitential intercession brought no appeasement to her misery.

II

DEEP WINTER

LEE WAS in Ian's flat, in the bath. Elaine had come round last night to listen to Bruno and Sam playing for a while, and then they had talked for a while longer, and as Elaine was clearly staying the night, Lee went to bed with Sam. In the morning he had left but Elaine seemed content to stay and play with the children so Lee left her to it and went round to Ian's to enjoy his running hot water.

She lay in the bath and fingered herself inside with a kind of appalled fascination. It felt like tripe. Lee had an image of a vivid yellow, spongy yet rigid, growth, already huge and still growing, hidden inside her. She imagined the doctor's look of horror at his sudden realisation as he exclaimed 'It's attached to her nervous system!' ('What does that mean, sir, was she in pain?' asks his white-coated assistant. 'Not so much pain, Bletchworth, more like a kind of bewildered misery, I should say, would be the way this would affect her.' 'O god, the poor woman.')

Lee pictured the crisp sheets of the hospital with longing. I'd love them to tuck me in tightly and turn out the light, she thought, knowing even as the words lined themselves up in her head that this was not true, and that if it ever happened, remembering that she had once claimed to long for it would be the worst irony of all.

That evening Lee fell asleep on the mattress during the evening and dreamed she was running away. She held her baby tight and as she ran, she held tight to the hand of her other child. The train was already in the station – it was starting – and

Lee flung herself into an open door as it suddenly, terrifyingly, gathered silent speed. She had not managed to hold the child close enough and now as Lee gripped his tiny hand she was still unable to pull him aboard and he hurtled alongside the train, his legs amazingly keeping pace and his little white face dogged and uncrying. The man opposite Lee leaned across and Lee thought with a lunge of relief, thank God, he will pull him aboard. But instead, the man with a sharp movement slammed the carriage door shut, breaking the child's arm. Lee woke with her own screams mingling with the screams of the dream until she realised it was all unreal, the colours and images that were so vivid a moment before were unreal, only the musty darkness of the night was real.

Lee was used to such dreams. Ever since she could remember, there were times when her mind overspilled with frighteningly filmic imagery of nightmare atrocities. Lee knew they were fantasies which did not exist except in the blitz of her overactive imagination. Except that they did, somewhere, and so did far worse: every imaginable scrap of suffering had happened sometime, every scared, scarred, face had existed somewhere, and every grotesque and violent tragedy that was a 'night terror' for her was real for someone. What was there to do during the long empty evenings but sit and cry.

It was just as difficult outside. Walked along the streets, staring down at their grimy slabs, Lee would find herself overwhelmed with the dreadfulness of this mass cementing the breathing earth. All progress is pollution, she thought, with such shuddering and total sense of comprehension that it amazed her how the turning world did not simply groan and cease, on that breath, its frantic activity. Moving past the rain-soaked litter of the Belfast gutters, it seemed to Lee that even the refuse was eloquent testament to the utter pointlessness of every human effort. She watched the sticky dust congealed in crevices along the paving stones with revulsion. The red, white, and blue paint splashes hurt her head. Someone had dropped a banana skin on the footpath, its limp and discomposing physicality a specifically real illustration of finite physical experience. But the banana skin was merely matter, it was not twisted by bomb blast into this graceless parody of its intended form, it had no death-crusted eyeballs, it gave no last shuddering cry of despair and lost hope, it was only a discarded banana skin going rotten. It held the horror of the world loosely, and let it gently spill.

This mood was not easy to live with. Lee's raw nerves quivered at every brusque moment in the world about her, and Bruno was becoming increasingly exasperated by her anguished eyes and cringing responses.

'You're bloody hysterical, woman,' he shouted one night when the unabating tension had rubbed them both raw again, 'I think you're going mad half the time.' The issue was unimportant, it had already escaped.

'If you think that, why don't you help me?'

'Help you! God, you're blinded with self pity aren't you? That's all you think about – you, you, you!'

'Don't be stupid Bruno.'

'I'm stupid, it doesn't matter what I try to do, I'm stupid, that's all you tell me.'

'Well what are you trying to do?'

Lee was shrieking now to match his shouts and there was a sharp bang at the back door.

'Go and see, I can't', Lee whispered, conscious now her face was streaked with mascara and swollen with tears.

'I've got no bloody boots on!'

'Then put your bloody boots on.'

Lee waited until he had struggled angrily into the first and then said 'Oh, what's the point. Whoever it was they'll be gone by now and we're not fit to see anyone anyway.'

Bruno threw the second boot towards Lee. It hit her shoulder and she yelped and collapsed. He picked it up and threw it at the window, which smashed. He retrieved the boot and left, punching Lee on the shoulder on his way out.

Lee screamed quietly in the empty room until interrupted by prolonged banging at the back door. She got up painfully and made her way down to the door. Five policemen stood there, lining the steps in their heavy wet capes and avid with intrusive indifference. Lee shuddered at the sight of the uniforms. She stood at the door controlling her sobs though she couldn't control the stream of tears that continued to drip.

'Just a barney?' asked the first policeman, scrutinising her. Lee nodded. He turned and called cheerfully behind him 'It's alright lads, just a barney.' But he came in anyway. They all came in, five big men in wet uniforms, perhaps bored by their night's patrol, prowling curiously around her kitchen, up the stairs to the living room where they stared at the window, and then at the psychedelic posters Lee had painted in homage to Alan Aldridge and the Beatles. Lee stood silent, absurd and humiliated in hot-pants and grim mask of grief, by the door, waiting for them to go away.

The policemen eventually returned to the back door. They did not comment on the overturned chair upstairs.

'Expect him back tonight?'

Lee nodded, having no idea whether she did or not.

'Give us a ring if he gives you any more bother,' said the policeman, and he retreated, leaving five times until the flat was emptied. Lee's ribs ached and she cried until Bruno returned later the same evening. He undressed her very gently and put her to bed where she cried herself to sleep with his hand gently on her although she was turned away from him.

Lee dreamed vividly of the end of the world. The entire dream was brilliantly coloured like an over-enhanced film sequence, but with the clarity of a Dali painting. She watched the huge mushroom cloud swell above the horizon to encompass the whole skyline, and recognised in herself the slow sad thought, well, that's it then, no escape. But it had been after all possible to escape: the violet-pink sky was full of the tiny balloons and parachutes of refugees, and the land had become engulfed with a curious iridescent liquid, upon which bobbed innumerable little boats, dotting the golden-speckled surface and looking, if one forgot the purpose of their frantic directionless flight, almost idyllic. It was not possible to forget, though. The dry unspeakable terror was locked into the dream. But she had escaped: she had found refuge with some monstrously misshapen creatures for whom the blast's mutation had been immediate. They had been transformed without evolution – they had ducks' heads, and snakes' tongues which licked and flickered as they spoke. They harboured Lee, told her of the worldwide destruction toll, which was of course immense. One of the molten lumps that had been bodies that they pointed out to her was Bruno, and in that instant of unbearable anguish as Lee realised she had abandoned him, without intention and without reflection, wilfully, ignorantly, to this fate, Lee woke abruptly. She felt charred with a misery so total that, trapped between the nightmare of her fantasy and the nightmare of her reality, she could only submit to a sense of boundless desolation.

Yes, she thought, it is all my fault, totally, everything. Everything that's gone wrong comes from me. I love Bruno but I'm relentlessly erasing our marriage, and replacing it with this senseless psychedelia of horror and anguish. I am to blame for all this.

Self-blame merges easily with self pity, and tears ease the way. Lee, who had prided herself for so long on walking away from her unhappy childhood, started indulging in random flashbacks. 'Sorry mummy' was the litany she remembered from her earliest childhood days, and 'Sorry isn't good enough' the regular response.

Once, when adolescent Lee had been sobbing after another of those furious, incomprehensible, rows with her mother, her father had approached her close enough to put his arm on hers, and Lee had reached across the silent gulf of unfamiliarity by wailing to him 'She makes me feel like a monster!' Her father had stroked her head, once, and said quietly 'You are not a monster.' He moved away then and left the room, but Lee had for a moment glimpsed the kind of comfort that another human being might have bestowed, that might have led to self-belief, and self-control. Is that it? she wondered now. Not a monster? Is that the best my childhood could give me to take away?

She remembered Melissa telling her that Aristotle had said 'Give me the child and I will show you the man.' They were talking about the segregation in Northern Irish education at the time, but Lee wondered now how she could have been so stupid as to think that by rejecting her home life she had crawled from under the all-embracing net to a place of perpetual safety.

Spring was slow coming and the cold was intensifying as the month went by. The fire in the living room glowed on all three bars from early morning till late at night, but they could still see their breath in the air. The electricity meter was taking nearly all of their scant resources, and Lee had to economise more and more on food, alternating suppers of 'rice curry' – rice with curry-powder-flavoured gravy – and 'potato stew' – boiled potatoes with oxo-flavoured gravy. Yet still the children whimpered with cold as icy scabs formed on the inside of the windows like frozen scurf. She piled coats on top of their blankets each night, but her teeth still chattered through the night and she woke stiff and shivering. Bath times had to be curtailed as, even though the plastic baby-bath was right beside the fireguard, her kettlefuls of water cooled as fast as she poured them in to fill it. Shopping trips were an ordeal in the biting wind, the little boy shivering silently beside her and the baby wailing thinly. *That child's foundered... that's a cold cry!* she would hear from the ever-informative matrons of Belfast she passed, and Lee longed to shout back *I know, you witch, we're all cold, we're all foundlings in this grim city hacked from Siberian slag*, but she gritted her chattering teeth and pushed on, fingers numb and pleated within her gloves, longing to be home and thawing her indigo toes, and longing for the end of these merciless days and shivering nights.

As the first signs of spring brought a chill sunshine, Lee took to walking round Botanic Gardens with Finn and Breff once again. When Melissa joined her on one such trip, Lee had been reminded of earlier times, with Ariadne. She started on a sad reflection but Melissa surprised her by interjecting 'Jesus, Lee, you couldn't stand the woman when she was alive. Why not admit it's actually a relief she's not around? Or is that against your religion?'

Lee turned in surprise. This from Melissa, who only a few weeks ago had assured her that everyone loved her. Melissa was smiling now, as though at a shaft of black humour. She continued in this mystifyingly jovial manner, 'Like your 'thing' about Paul – you didn't even particularly like him, you were just piqued that he sneaked out of your magic matrix!'

This made no sense at all to Lee, but it sounded uncomfortably as though Melissa had chosen those words carefully, each one designed to provoke her to protestations and discussion. She stood silently for a moment.

'You have to make a friend of everyone you meet, that's your trouble,' Melissa went on, in a tone of conciliation that only added to Lee's confusion. To her, a wide circle of friendship was an admirable thing, but Melissa didn't sound at all admiring.

Lee hesitated, still confused. Then she said, 'You know I just like talking to people, Melissa. "A stranger is just a friend you haven't met." '

She made little bunny ears in the air to show she was self-parodying, to take the sting out of this unexpected conversation.

Melissa's smile evaporated as she responded, apparently exasperated, 'Say that to the guys stoning the flats in the Falls, Lee, and see if they drop their rocks and go back to the Shankill.'

Lee turned back to the path and pushed stubbornly on.

She felt hurt, but not deterred. There had to be a way through the extremes. There had to be undemanding friendships, there was no other way to peace. She focussed her gaze on the beds of roses, newly planted for the upcoming exhibition, now in bud but still too tightly closed to see what colour they would bloom.

What Lee feared was that she and Melissa were losing their precious intimacy. Not that Melissa was withdrawing but because Lee had realised, reluctantly, that her friend's probing analysis would bring no comforting comprehension. 'I've been hung up about Paul since that night,' she had confided initially, hoping calm analysis might steady her spinning world, but instead felt repelled by Melissa's eagerness for details. 'I can't explain,' she kept repeating, 'I don't know why. I'm just a bit hung up about Paul.'

'It's understandable,' Melissa had decided, 'I mean, if you've had good sex with someone, you want it again – so go for it! I always do. I'm quite ruthless, I just go for what I want.'

Lee knew such feedback was not what she needed. She didn't even want to repeat her night with Paul, and certainly not to pursue him. What she wanted was to find some rationale for her over-reaction – if not why he had disappeared from her life, at least why she minded so much – why everything was unravelling around her. Bruno had always been her stability, but she couldn't say to him, *'Bruno I've got myself a bit hung up on Paul, and it's really getting to me that he won't speak to me now,'* and talk through the night until everything was alright again, she thought. I can't expect him to recreate me. I have to do it myself.

Gradually it began to seem less as if the axis of her world had shifted momentously and more as if there had simply been another extension in their agreed definition of the ties of marriage. She hadn't expected to fall stupidly in love with someone who didn't reciprocate, but she hadn't made any plans to avoid it either. She had focussed on ensuring the 'bonds of marriage' never chafed her. Why, she had argued, should marriage mean living in each others' pockets, sewn up like kittens in a bag for drowning – full-grown foetuses struggling to achieve siamese-twinning? It was absurd, and frustrating for both partners, to suppose that marriage must mean the end of personal choice and autonomous thought. 'We have made a structure to survive, we will explore it logically and intelligently,' Lee had explained once to Melissa, 'but that doesn't mean we're not as caring of each other as before – probably we are more so, because we're aware of ourselves in a new way and not just following a social duty.'

But now, Melissa's avid, analytical, responses were neither comforting nor illuminating. And besides, she knew Melissa's current 'ruthless target' was Bruno, and she was beginning to feel uncomfortable in these conversations.

Maybe the doctor's prescription helped, or perhaps she simply became bored with her own self-pity but as the days stretched into weeks, the effort of stealing herself in case she met Paul and then reconciling herself to not meeting him, became less obsessive. She felt less guilty about her moods now Bruno had become less exasperated with her, and was beginning to realise that this was mostly because he had the constant support of Elaine. Lee was grateful as this eased her guilt, and felt full of respect for the way they both managed their relationship. When they were together in the flat, Lee felt neither excluded nor patronised, and Elaine's friendship was a steady consolation in the debris of the crumpled structure of her marriage. With the help of this strong friendship, Lee felt sure she and Bruno would be able to rebuild their own relationship with new understanding and on firmer foundations.

As the tensions outside mounted, their now-regular Saturday night parties seemed like sanctuaries against the anger in the city. Lee and Bruno's flat had become the hub for these gatherings and there were still times when it felt like the great experiment she had always intended it to be – a brave, reckless, enquiry into the unknown capabilities and strength of human love. *'We had this fine old place in the country – where we grew marijuana on the lawn – fornicating all night long..'* Bruno would sing in the smoke-filled living room to the group crouched round him, nodding at the sombre songs, shouting with laughter at the jests. Lee had so much wanted their city flat to be that fine old place. She had wanted to reclaim glamour in decadence, to enhance the cynicism around their socially-defined poverty with defiant style – to identify with creative indulgence.

Bruno was developing his playing techniques. Tonight he was exploring twelve bar blues on a borrowed Yamaha to extend his repertoire of performance. Lee watched him, envying him that simple connection to the moment, undistracted by the small audience gathering around him, remaining engrossingly absorbed in the song. She shook her head to scatter the introspection and moved from the listening group to the dancing group in the other room.

Pressed rat and wart-hog have closed down their shop
They didn't want to, it was all they had got...

Lee was in her own obsessive thread now, dancing in a close isolation, raptly attentive to the sweet murky sub-world of Cream's music. A male figure claimed her from the blurred dark. It was necessary to move rhythmically, seductively, to the seductive rhythm, and perhaps later it would be necessary to climb the coat-crammed, indifferent, stairs to the bedroom and there continue a rhythmic motion.

Tonight's paramour was Nathan, Josh's younger brother, newly arrived in Belfast and avid, it seemed to Lee, to join their group. As they danced their way closer to inevitability he surprised her by whispering conspiratorially 'It's all his idea really, isn't it?'

Lee knew that was not true, but had no desire to explain. She didn't want to go to the place that his question had taken her, where she knew the true answer was: *It was my idea, actually*

– *I wanted to live like this.* It had been so important, once, to believe she was choosing something honest and important. She had loved being the earth-mother figure of the group – the one with sons – and perhaps most arrogant of all, she had believed their philosophy could somehow slowly saturate this angry, hate-filled, city, and show that people were not born Prods or Micks but just small mammals reaching out for love. All this had been bombed out now by her own mismanagement and by that, faded now but still toxic, obsession with Paul.

The mood in the city was changing and the difference was beginning to show. Friends still called round daily, but the talk was increasingly laced with comment on the growing dangers in the streets. 'Are you not worried about living above a newsagents?' Josh asked, in between a session of republican songs one evening.

'Ah but your man Smith is a protestant, his name's above the door,' Bruno had responded quickly, not looking across to where Lee sat. He picked up his guitar and wedged his smouldering cigarette in the top strings, ready for a quick drag between verses, 'Anyone playing? I'm in E.'

But Mr Smith is not here at nights, Lee thought. It's just us. And that threatening scrawl that creeps back onto our wall. The next time she went out using the shop's front door, she took a long look at the wide letter box where the daily newspapers were pushed through early in the morning to be marked up for delivery. Wide enough for a very large parcel. How big was a parcel bomb? She had been glad no painted union jacks were adorning their wall when they first arrived, but as troubles escalated, Lee realised she would feel safer if they had been.

Tension in the city was increasingly visible, yet it had a sense of the absurd about it, as though taking it seriously wasn't the way this resilient city dealt with threat. Bruno had been on a college placement one day when a bomb alert had resulted in the army arriving in his classroom to check it out. 'They asked if we'd seen a bomb,' he reported, marvelling, 'as if it was a lost pup, or something. Of course all the lads took a chance to dive under their desks and mess about, checking cupboards, and generally making a disruption. The uniforms just stayed in the doorway, waiting, until our lads said it was all clear, and then they said 'Thanks' and they left. I mean... really? A bunch of laddos from the Shankill and Falls say there's no bomb, so it's OK?'

They laughed, because on that occasion it was OK. But bomb threats were part of daily life now and it was getting harder to find the funny side of a city that increasingly defined itself as a war zone. Later that week Bruno came home with a more serious tale. He'd reached Shaftesbury Square on his way home from his placement and found soldiers blocking the entrance to Donegal Pass, and sniper fire coming from the Lisburn Road. Lee's local geography was still unclear on road names, but she had seen enough images of the crouching, running, figures and retaliatory uniforms to get the picture.

'The army were returning the attack from behind their Saracens, and I'd somehow wandered into the middle of it,' Bruno said, pulling a Silk Cut from his pack with fingers that still looked to Lee a little bit quivery. 'I think I did vaguely hear some Brit officer-type voice shouting 'Stop' a few times, and then 'Get down!' How was I to know he was shouting at me? As far as I was concerned, it was just another bloody patrol throwing their weight around. Anyway, I scuttled off and cowered in a chemist's doorway 'til it was all over, then headed for home. I could kill for a coffee, Lee, love.'

Lee found herself gravitating more often to Dervla's house now. It was easier, because she could take the children, who seemed always contented to play quietly in the big kitchen which was warmer from its steady-burning Aga than any of the rooms in Lee and Bruno's flat. Lee tried to remember to bring some contribution, even if it was only grapes or a few tomatoes from the market, as Dervla was generous with fresh-made oatcakes, ginger biscuits, and other home-made treats. Lee's conversation tended to begin with appreciative thanks which she tried to stop from meandering into introspective self-deprecation. She was pretty sure that while this would have lured Melissa into intriguing personal analysis, Dervla found it boring.

'What do you plan to do yourself, then?' she had asked, rather brusquely, handing Lee her mug of coffee.

Lee knew Dervla had made and fired the pottery mug as well grinding the coffee, and had planned to praise her for both activities, but she felt stalled.

'I haven't any plans – or any skills, really –'
Dervla could clearly sense an admiring comparison on its way, and interrupted.

'Would you not train to do something yourself?'

'Oh…' Direct questions about her intentions tended to baffle Lee. I never know the answers, she thought ruefully. 'Like what?' she asked.

'Anything. You should look at the brochures of what's around.'

'Well the boys are so little –'

'There's evening classes, Lee, you live near enough and it's not as if you're stuck for babysitters – everyone's falling over themselves to hang around at your place.'

It occurred to Lee now that Dervla didn't have a similarly busy social scene around her despite the splendid creativity of her own place. She felt fleetingly sorry for her, just for long enough to distract her from considering the question. Yes, she could take some course – not just yet, but some time, and she would get herself a career sorted.

Dervla was still watching her and, she realised, still waiting for her to say something grown-up and sensible. 'I'd like to do something with art…' Lee suggested eventually. She immediately sensed a sharpened scrutiny from Dervla, whose painted stools and tables, she knew, were commissioned by a furniture shop in Grafton street where Tom drove regularly to deliver them. 'With children,' she added quickly, and Dervla's look softened.

'You should do that,' she said. 'You're good with the kids. Mine like you, they love it when you read to them.'

'Really? I make up lots of it you know, it's mainly pictures in the books – I look out to see which bits make their eyes go wide.'

'That's the Irish way,' Dervla said, and they both laughed.

Now that she was dropping in on Dervla more often, Lee was beginning to realise that most of the marriages that appeared to be operating traditionally were, though more privately perhaps, just as loosely linked and untethered as their own. In the molten times of these nights of distant gunshots and closer street-fights, monogamy no longer seemed as part of the marital structure for their group. Dervla confided, quite casually, that she had a lover in London, where she intermittently escaped. She had to lie to Tom, she explained to Lee, by making pretexts for the visits and pretending she was staying with her sister. She was envious of Lee and Bruno's life-style.

'How do you manage to keep it so civilised?' she asked Lee. Lee started to feel self-conscious at the realisation their life-style was being widely talked about, and wondered how their activities were reported. With contempt? With compassion? Dervla anyway seemed to find it all something to be admired.

'Tom would kill me if he knew about my fella,' Dervla confided.

'Don't you feel bad that he doesn't know?' Lee asked, belatedly aware she sounded both naive and smug. Dervla was unfazed.

'Not at all. I just wish he was hiding some wee bit on the side, but he isn't. He's really straight. He believes we should just stick to each other, all the time – he gets terribly jealous at parties.' She giggled, then sighed. 'He won't dance with anyone else, just stands and glowers at me while I'm having fun. I get so mad. Bruno's not like that, is he.'

'No, he's not.' Lee acknowledged. Braggingly, she added 'So far from it, in fact, that I took them both up breakfast in bed this morning.'

Dervla burst into a pleat of giggles and put her hand over her mouth to contain them, staring big-eyed over the top of her fingers at Lee.

'Them! Him and who? Elaine?' Lee nodded, delighted herself by her own unconventionality.

'Oh god no, that could never happen here,' sighed Dervla, then 'But don't you get jealous?'

'Oh, no.' said Lee seriously, then joined in quickly with Dervla's giggles. But no, that foggy helpless feeling was not jealousy, she knew that. So much was meaningless, but some things at least were clear and certain. Those moments this morning, when the three of them had sat on the bed together, drinking coffee and eating toast while the children sat watching Sunday morning cartoons downstairs – Elaine in just her dressing-gown, Bruno in jeans, and Lee fully dressed – that was real. There had been a gentle sense of giving and accepting then that did not scratch and scar. From these small moments, a pattern might perhaps begin to grow.

12

SPRING

I T WAS GETTING HARDER to find sense and calm in Belfast. The cold that had gripped the city was ebbing now, overtaken by a late spring – not exactly warm, but close. There was an atmosphere of grimy heat on the streets, a stickiness about the dust, and a smell of quicker deterioration around the garbage in the back alleys. And even a hint of summer on its way had racked the hostilities up another notch. The Protestant back streets were wreathed once again with their tatty red white and blue bunting, councillors and politicians argued about whether the marches should be stopped or allowed, and the shootings went on. Attitudes were hardening and everyone seemed agreed on one thing only – that the media were making everything worse, their reporters were either intractable or gullible, and they were creating alliances by the power of their headlines and the emphasis of their photographs. People seemed over-reactive generally, not just politically, though perhaps both were linked. Josh's brother Nathan, after just three weeks in Belfast, had swallowed a bottleful of aspirins feeling he couldn't cope. The hospital, unsympathetic in a casualty ward full of the relics of civil conflict, had pumped his stomach out and sent him away next day, but his family were disgusted with him and wouldn't have him back.

'It's no good showing them pity,' Josh had said, shocking Lee by including his own sibling in the loose category of those desperate enough to try to take their own life, 'They only do it for attention.'

'But if he did something as drastic as that to show how

much he needs attention, shouldn't we give him some?' Lee argued. Ariadne swam vaguely into her mind, struggling and submerging in the dark river. Josh was adamant, but Bruno agreed with Lee so Nathan came to stay with them while he 'convalesced'. His ordeal seemed to have left him with a mix of dejected hypochondria and eccentric high spirits, which Lee found puzzling but so much was baffling these days she didn't suspect, at the time, this too might prove explosive. But she could not soothe her own jarring confusion vicariously through calming Nathan. He remained uncalm, and after a while disappeared back into the city. Lee found she could not grieve that he too had left the past unatoned.

It wasn't all bad, of course. It wasn't all fear and neurosis. Spring made them all more mobile, and the days became again a stream of visitors from, and visits to, the wide cast around her that Lee used to reassure herself that their lives were brimful of friendship and activity. There was always someone else at the flat. People seemed to call round whenever they felt like a daytime party, confident they would not be the only visitors. Elaine spent a lot of her free time there: she made them meals, and continued creating clothes for the children. Bruno got the baby-bouncer out again and fixed it in the doorway, now there was enough warmth without the door closed and the baby was old enough to support his head and back. Breff's delight was enchanting. His eyes dilated with excitement and his newly-discovered crawling skill seemed to accelerate – his fast-forward mode, Bruno called it – whenever he saw his father hooking it up in the doorway. He never tired of jerking up and down in it, dribbling with laughter, and Finn would stand by him ready to gently jiggle it when his little brother seemed to be flagging.

Lee bought a film for her Kodak Instamatic and started photographing the flat frequently, with its wide range of visitors, as if to prove to herself these friendships were not imaginary. The snaps were mostly taken indoors with flash since the flat had no garden, only the back yard with its dustbins and steep iron staircase, but on warmer days they would open the living-room window and some of their braver friends would clamber onto the broad ledge of windowsill above the shop and perch there precariously. No-one was allowed to take the children out there, of course, but when Bruno clambered outside with his guitar, Lee would stand close to the window holding the boys on a chair so they could watch and listen. Both loved this, and appeared to have some secret 'dare you' game going on between them, looking across at each other giggling then suddenly lurching forward as if about to jump, pulling immediately back with more giggles. Melissa had explained to her that Breff couldn't possibly have the spatial awareness that would be necessary for him to comprehend such a tease, but Lee privately demurred. The brothers were extraordinarily close, and she was sure they communicated in secret ways.

Their street was still considered fairly safe, as it had no organised iconography like the Red Hand of Ulster, only sectarian scrawls, but elsewhere in the city massive street murals were marking out battle grounds and the newspapers were full of photographs of soldiers: Soldiers patrolling, their green and black camouflage kit standing out strangely against the red brick and grey facades of the Belfast streets. Soldiers crouching behind cars or being shouted at by children or stoned by teenagers. Soldiers clashing with protesters, batons out and shields up. Soldiers gazing at debris after bombings, looking humanly bewildered and sad. Lee was used to the 'mixed race' community around the university and although she realised there were seriously defined enclaves of Protestants and Catholics, she had been slow to recognise which areas of the city defined themselves as Orange areas and which as Sinn Fein. Graffiti and flags were increasingly marking out these territories unmistakably. Both groups had vigilante squads – for peace-keeping, she had hoped, and was shocked when The Ploughman's Head, Catholic-owned although in a mixed area, was bombed and the UVF took proud responsibility.

'Good for employment, though,' said Josh cheerily, 'There's a whole new job opportunity in the city now.'

Lee stared, baffled by his smile as much as his news. Josh was quick to clarify:

'Rear gunner on the milk floats.'

She laughed half-heartedly, but Bruno responded more seriously. 'Aye, well, they'll need to start putting the white stuff in cartons soon – those bottles are favourite with both sides.' Lee knew he meant for the petrol bombs that seemed part of the life in the city now.

'Seriously, though,' Bruno went on, 'It's changing out there. There's always been scuffles at chucking-out time but some nights it's like marching season already, without waiting for the Orange Day parades. I remember when I was a kid there was a big scuffle at the top of our road – after a footie match, I guess – and one of our neighbours was stranded on the wrong side of it. They literally stopped the fight to escort her through – parted like the Red Sea – and once she was safe at her doorway, the fists were flying again and battle resumed. You wouldn't see that these days.'

Josh agreed, unfazed by his nostalgia. 'No way. He'd be kneecapped for consorting with the enemy,' he said, adding after a moment's thought 'And she'd never wear that coat again, for fear he'd dusted it with explosives.'

Lee didn't even laugh that time.

That was the week they heard about 'Orange Lil' on Radio Free Ulster up in the Shankill Road, one of the tranche of pirate radio stations on both sides of the divide currently regularly broadcasting taunts and threats, who had played 'Are You Lonesome Tonight?' after the death of a Catholic youth, saying it was a special request for his mother.

'Black-hearted bitch,' said Bruno, and he held Lee and let her sob on his chest.

It seemed that a different rhythm, a quieter one, might be settling on their personal lives, as the shadows of the gunmen stalked the streets. And then on one particular night, as the evening was darkening and the soldiers were setting up the road blocks outside, Lee had got into a conversation about marriage. Guy had been joking to Rowena and Josh about their upcoming wedding day.

'How soon before the car-keys are on the table at your dinner-parties, eh?' he had said, wagging his head, and Lee had joined the laughter without really knowing why, until the gags about 'swinging' followed. It hadn't really occurred to Lee before that her commitment to create a loving community of extended family could be mistaken for something so seedy, greedy, and gross. She remembered making a jokey quip about wife-swapping, ages ago, but that was nothing to do with their own careful structure of open marriage, creating a community of freedom to love without social stigma. Something within her cringed, half-humiliated, half-indignant, and she hung around in the kitchen for a chance to join the conversation again.

It came when Guy declared to the bride-to-be 'Well, I wish you both all the best but a good marriage is frankly impossible.'

'Society makes impossible demands on the marriage structure,' Lee said quickly, 'but that doesn't mean you can't adapt them.'

Guy demurred. 'It's not the fault of society, it's human nature. Successful marriage is simply an impossible idea, by definition. It's literally not possible for two human beings to live together without giving up their individuality – at least one of them must, usually it's both. And if we're going to grow, we need to be individuals.'

'Yes, true – but I don't agree that you can't grow within a permanent relationship,' Lee responded earnestly. 'The problem is, so many people respond to any tension in the marriage in the stereotypical way our society has decreed. So if there's any stress, they don't check out their actual feelings, they just pick from the list of what's expected – indignation, grievance, resentment, that sort of thing – when perhaps they don't really feel that way at all. They have feelings of course, but they think these have to be stereotypical responses just because they've submitted to a marriage – they follow a social rule rather than remembering that other person's feelings and needs were once as important to them as their own.'

'Hold on a minute, Lee,' Guy said when she finally paused, 'If there's all that, grievance and resentment and whatever else you said, then there is a real problem. And it's human nature, not marriage, that gets people uptight when they have a problem. So if one person gets attracted to someone else, the one they are with is going to feel hurt and upset. What are they supposed to do about it?'

Lee had cut in before he finished. 'They're not necessarily going to feel upset. Feeling attracted to someone else is practically inevitable, so why decide to feel hurt when it happens?'

Guy was shaking his head. 'You don't 'decide' to feel hurt, it's what happens when your marriage partner goes with someone else –'

'But that's just what I'm saying, it doesn't need to. If marriage has anything to offer, it should withstand that.'

'And yet it can't. Marriage is an impossible ideal. You're arguing for me, not against me.' Guy's voice had softened, like he was suddenly sad and sorry for her. Lee stared at him puzzled. She knew she had not explained herself very well, and tried again.

'But if you love someone and you want to make a family with them, then it's good to stay together to care for your young ones – most creatures do that.'

'Not lions.' This was from Josh, who had returned with Rowena and their replenished mugs of ale. 'Mum gets the cubs out of dad's way in case he kills them. I'm a Leo, by the way.'

Lee ignored Rowena's giggles and continued, focusing on Guy: '– so by combining child-rearing and personal freedom, an open marriage is ideal.'

He laughed. 'Open marriage isn't an ideal, it's an oxymoron. Marriage is a union, which means a joining of two into one. The breaking of that union bond is infidelity – or, if repeated, philandering. Opening doesn't come into it.'

'Anything is an ideal if you want it, and make it work.'

Lee was beginning to feel wretched now, and struggling not to take his comments as derisory criticism of her personally. 'Polygamy is just as valid as monogamy in lots of parts of the world,' she went on, stumbling, and she knew she'd lost the argument then.

'Oh aye, and so is child marriage, and slave ownership – and female circumcision for that matter. What are you advocating in the name of universal equality now, Lee? Intimacy is precious, why do you want to stretch it like bubble-gum and hand it round to everyone?'

'And anyway, if children are involved,' Rowena put in, 'the marriage has got to be unbreakable, for their security.'

'Security doesn't come from monogamy,' Lee countered, 'Like Guy says, it's impossible to promise that you'll never be attracted by someone else, ever again, but he thinks the answer is not to get married. I think the answer is to accept that marriage includes that option, not to ban it. I believe it's possible to enjoy sexual encounters within a marriage. I know you think I'm being naïve, Guy, but it's important to redefine our personal roles if we're ever going to manage redefining society.'

He took another swig of spirit and gave a small sigh. 'Not so much naïve, Lee as deluding yourself. You can't keep what we're calling "attraction" on the side like a hobby – suppose one of the partners falls properly in love?'

'I don't know,' said Lee, then, as he looked at her steadily, 'I suppose you have to ride it out. You both have to accept it's happening, and … ride it out. The marriage has to stretch to hold even that.'

Guy placed his hand gently on her arm. 'It can't be done,'

he said simply. 'It can't be done.'

'Marriage is a sanctuary,' said Rowena, 'and it ought to stay that way. People can't go on doing whatever they want, once they're married. Marriage changes everything – it's serious, it's a sanctuary.'

Lee could not answer Rowena's wide-eyed, slightly slurred, imploring statement of belief. She knew Rowena was a bit pissed and meant to say 'sacrament' and she knew that what Rowena believed in was something she herself had long ago dismissed. The word-slip, which Rowena's earnest, entreating, gaze suggested she had still not noticed, seemed strangely apt. That's how we are taught to use marriage, she thought, as a sanctuary. That means refuge, doesn't it. A place where you're protected, and you can't be pursued any more, not because there is any intrinsic protection there but simply because everyone has agreed that's how it shall be. Only it's a very savage sanctuary, because a refuge should be a shelter, and this place is more of a maze – a kind of labyrinth where you go on endlessly and you don't even know where you're going. There must be some place that's safe, between losing your identity and breaking up your relationship, but you can't find it in the dark. You just go on and on, hoping and trusting, and you might be destroying everything.

Guy and Rowena were still watching her. She tried again.

'If you believe in trust, it must be unconditional. You can't just say, 'I trust you to do *this*, and not to do *that*.' It's got to be, 'I trust you, whatever you do.' Because you can't know what's going to happen in your marriage.'

Guy continued to smile at her and sip from his hip-flask, but Rowena had now turned back to Josh for a private, nonverbal, conversation. As she was about to move on, Guy put his arm on hers unexpectedly. 'You know how many hedonists it takes to change a light bulb? None! They're all too busy enjoying the darkness.'

He moved away laughing, leaving Lee feeling oddly numb.

Hedonist, is that what he thought of her brave crusade to bring connection to this city of blades and bombs? When had Guy started to judge her? She had thought him an admiring observer, but now in the shadowy stairwell it seemed he was only ever an amused flaneur, watching quietly as Loki watched Baldur, knowing he had shaped the mistletoe spear that would inevitably murder his friend.

Lee started to feel a little shaky. She wondered if she should have a lie down but the party was in her house and the bedrooms were sure to be full. Sometimes she felt so so sure this was the only way to live, emancipated and rational – she could genuinely believe that she and Bruno really did have something valuable to offer the world. She decided to join the dancing, but a voice from the shadows said quietly 'Have you ever thought what effect your lifestyle might have on your children?'

Lee turned and recognised the man she had met at Melissa's party – the one whose wife complained about her child reaching the 'terrible twos.' Why is he even in my house, she thought, irrationally annoyed, and held out her paper cup towards his bottle defiantly before replying. She struggled to find words to respond as if this was a genuine enquiry, not a scathing put-down.

'I believe,' she said carefully, '– we both believe, that children need a loving environment to survive and thrive, and deserve more than just two adults, or even one, for this. They need to feel part of a family and part of a community too. We'll always love them the most, of course, but the more people around them who have a nurturing relationship with them, the more emotionally healthy they will become.'

He stared without smiling. She remembered now he was a sociology lecturer.

'The community around here' he said, gesturing beyond the room but still staring at her intently, 'is very strong on family values. You may have noticed.'

Lee knew he was jeering at her but she took a deep breath.

'Yes,' she said, and what this city needs is an antidote to all the hostility and prejudice that's thick as the grime of the streets around here – barricades at every corner, men with guns and kids with stones, and tribal colours painted on the bricks and fences and anger everywhere. Rules and religion can't help – they're what fuels this mess. The only thing mankind needs to survive and thrive, beyond physical sustenance, is love.'

She was shaking now. He was still staring at her and they seemed to be alone.

'Are you confusing multiple shagging with love?' he said, and she had not expected him to say anything crude so she stared back for a moment without replying, The silence stretched and then she said quietly

'You've changed the question. The question should be, do I believe that intimate loving shared freely, in transgression of every man-made rule about official permission, could help create a community that's kinder, and less prejudiced – then the answer is yes. Yes, I do.'

He seemed unable to decide whether to shake his head in disagreement or nod in exasperation, as he appeared to be doing both. Then he said 'Why marry, though? I mean if your message to the world is simply Make Love Not War, why complicate things by getting married?'

Lee wanted to say, because a commitment to stay together was part of the big experiment, because we wanted to be grown-ups and show that grown-ups can do things differently, because we had a baby coming and needed to find somewhere to live in a city full of bigots, because it was a protest, a challenge, and a wedding was a chance to party. It seemed to her that all those things, while true, were not really reasons that would make much sense to this man. As the silence lengthened once again, Lee wondered if they really made much sense to her, either.

Lee left the group on the stairs and went up to the bedroom to check on the boys. Finn had taken to crying when the introductory music to the news came on the television. 'And now, Northern Ireland,' the toneless voice of the newscaster would say, and the familiar images of violence would flicker on to the screen while details beyond the children's comprehension were intoned in corroboration to the debris and carnage. Breff was still frequently sick too, especially after rain brought the debris of the weekend's CS gas bombardment, but tonight they were both quiet and breathing gently in sleep.

She went back downstairs to the party for a while. She was glad to see Melissa had taken a rare break from her all-engrossing thesis and was one of a small group moving voluptuously to *Bridge over Troubled Water* on the Dansette. Melissa was sufficiently intrigued by Lee's tense expression to abandon the dance and steer her out to the quiet hall.

'Now come on, tell me what's wrong' she began, sounding to Lee uncomfortingly jubilant. 'Who is it this time? And why isn't your infallible charm working?'

'It's not that...' Lee felt almost too mortified by her friend's assumption of her predatory motivation to respond at all, and quickly wished she hadn't bothered to try as Melissa responded 'Oh come on – we all get pissed off when lust is thwarted!'

Melissa was laughing but Lee wasn't in the mood either to think carnally or even to deny it. Lee feared she was close to losing something precious in her life: the ideal she had lived by seemed to be disintegrating. And now it seemed that Melissa had never understood what her marriage with Bruno meant to them both. All around them, tribal bonds and clan divisions had created hatred, violence, assault and death, and they had held out for something else. Love, not the christ-god that both sides had erected on a burning cross, but palpable, visceral, ongoing daily love. Connection at its most intimate and honest, and vulnerable. If that's eliminated, the world goes insane.

Lee murmured something indistinct and fetched her coat and went out of the back door, climbing quickly down the precariously steep iron steps that caused so much bother with the children and so much worry as to how they would get out if they were under petrol bomb attack, and out into the back alley. She ran with no clear intention until the road blocks drew her back to awareness and she walked more cautiously for a while, then stopped, indecisive. Ian Kingston lived just off this street, in his self-consciously arty flat decorated mainly with matt black paint. It seemed to Lee now that Ian might be the person to turn to. She had no emotional involvement with him, he was clever and therefore might turn out to be wise and, even more than anyone else she knew, he liked to talk. Maybe his precise, pedantic, world view would put everything into a less emotional perspective. She rang the bell and was admitted.

Ian was alone. He seemed shocked, and asked 'What's wrong?'

His concern was obvious, but Lee realised she had no idea what the answer was, other than that she had talked a lot about marriage and got herself into a state. She started to cry and Ian became visibly uneasy. Perhaps relying on the social formula that had sufficed as communication between them in the past, he offered her a bath. Lee started to laugh, still crying, and then as Ian seemed really bothered now, she quickly calmed down and accepted a coffee and sat quietly for a while in Ian's study. She envied the dark peacefulness of the room, its shelves all crammed with the close and ordered activity of Ian's life. Precision and control ruled that room, perhaps a little ruffled now by Lee's disorderly presence, but ready to regain possession as soon as this unimportant intrusion was over. Lee saw all this, and stopped wishing Ian would say something comforting, and felt a consolation in his inability to talk to her. The only answer was, of course, what she had known since she was a child: you are on your own. Get on with it.

'No, Ian, it's not Bruno. Bruno is fine, we are fine. It's just me.'

'Do you want…?' He was peering at her, pointing to the phone.

Even Ian's phone was dark and smooth and sleekly shaped.

Its alien shape seemed absurdly apt. She felt quite steady now.

'We're not on the phone. It's ok, I'm ok now. Sorry to bother you so late, and.. er, thanks for the coffee.'

The party was still going on when she got back, and the back door opened at her knock without comment by a student who was draining a keg of bitter into a cup in the sink. They didn't recognise each other but both smiled.

Elaine was supposed to be visiting the next evening but she didn't arrive. Bruno called round to see what had happened and found her subdued and evasive. Ian had been having a word with her, he reported on his return, and had 'warned her off' – she was 'upsetting Lee,' he said. Bruno had assured her this wasn't true and talked her into coming round.

'I was right wasn't I?' he said to Lee, looking serious and slightly troubled.

'I just went out for a quick turn for a breath of air, then I thought I heard some commotion,' Lee said, anxious to reassure them, and realising as she spoke that this was actually not untrue.

Elaine nodded. 'There were riots in the Shankhill last night,' she confirmed, 'I heard about it on the radio this morning.'

'Well I couldn't tell where it was,' Lee said, 'but I was near Ian's then… I only stayed for a quick coffee.' That at least was all true, and it was true too when she said to Elaine, 'Honestly, I love you coming round here, I would really mind it if you stopped coming. Ian just doesn't know us very well.'

Elaine seemed reassured and Bruno relieved, and Lee, paranoid about never lying, was glad that she had said nothing untruthful, though the discussion disconcerted her and she felt diminished and slightly humiliated, like some cumbersome older person on a charabanc outing who has to be helped down the step. But they all spent a gentle, companionable evening together, and everything seemed back to normal.

Lee wrote later that night in her journal

What is promiscuity? Is it unselective copulation? That's what most animals do. Why do humans introduce selection? There is a kind of natural selection from our sequence of encounters, but why shouldn't this sphere be open to experimentation as much as any other sphere of human activity – like cookery, or literature? You don't know what you like till you try, and if our moral code is valid, it can withstand questioning. If it's intrinsically wrong to be what we call 'promiscuous' this will be proven by bad outcomes. Like unhappiness. But if no-one is unhappy, then it's only our socially-manufactured sense of guilt that divides wrong from right. If you can behave as you choose and not feel guilty about it, it's not wrong. But if you postulate an abstract moral code, then that code can't be transgressed without recrimination and this reinforces the sense of committing wrong. So morality is a self-generating concept, promiscuity is a life-choice not a sin, and the only truly moral conclusion is not to falter.

Lee studied this summary of her mental paradox for a while and then added underneath, impulsively *Do I ever feel guilty? Once, never. Now, all the time.*

13

BROWN SUGAR AND SPILT COFFEE

A ND THEN a termination, of sorts, came eventually and violently, provided by Cara. It came, of course, after a party. Was there anything but parties and listening out for trouble in those days, Lee wondered later.

The gathering point was Tim and Siobhan's flat and the usual crowd was there including the Brothers Grimm, as Lee always mentally called them since the story of the pre-nuptial beatings. They were both in solemn mood that night, as there'd been news of a civilian shot by the army in the Lower Falls during the day. 'Only twenty-one, he was,' said the younger brother, 'no older than meself. Shot during disturbances, they're saying – sure, he'll go down in the bastards' records as another IRA man nailed.'

'He'll be another Gerard McAuley so,' the elder one said bitterly, and there were murmurs of assent. The group around the brothers began to talk sadly and angrily, and Bruno had taken Lee out to the kitchen for a refill.

'Who was that, Gerard …?' Lee wanted to know when it seemed safe to ask. She had forgotten the surname, but Bruno knew.

'That's two years ago, when the army first came in and the old biddies were still giving the lads in uniform cups of tea and thinking they'd come to protect them. The McAuley boy was helping some Catholics evacuate a bad area, up near Bombay Street I think, and he was shot by a Protestant sniper. It was a big thing at the time. The authorities blamed it all on the IRA but it turned out the lads had only a pitiful few weapons to hold back the attacks, and in the end the whole street got burned out. The soldiers stood by and did nothing, and the B Specials joined in the attacks.'

'Why wasn't that in the English papers?' Lee demanded, near to tears -'why wasn't it news all over the world?'

Bruno handed her one of the tinnies he'd rustled from under the table. 'Here, take this and be glad we're alive yet,' he toasted her as he clipped top for her, and they touched cans before returning to the room where sounds of *Brown Sugar* showed the dancing had begun.

Lee joined in but she couldn't shake her sombre mood and when round about midnight, their host said to her as a joke in passing 'What will we do when Melissa finishes her thesis? Parties won't be the same without your dancing,' although she laughed and answered quickly 'Actually, she loves baby-sitting – she says it saves on her electricity bill and Finn is the most entertaining conversationalist of all her acquaintances', she decided she wanted to go. Bruno was ready as he'd come without his guitar that night and there were no musicians to join, so they got their coats.

James had arrived quite late, on his own, but as Lee and Bruno made their move to leave with Elaine, he decided he was off too and offered to run them home. Fionnula was at her mother's for the weekend, James said. 'Why?' Lee asked. 'Why do you think,' responded James, and drove them back to her and Bruno's flat. Bruno and Elaine got out.

'We'll go back to my place' James said to Lee. He drove the car at furious speed through the Belfast streets. Once they were checked at a military road block, but they were waved on. It was after two a.m. Lee realised with a feeling of foreboding that James's route was taking him back past the party – that he was in fact drawing up opposite Tim and Siobhan's door.

'What's this for?' she asked.

'I'll just see if Paul and Cara are coming.' His grin seemed both vacuous and inscrutable. Lee controlled a tremor of panic.

'James, they're not – Paul won't come if I'm here.'

James laughed and kissed her. With a desperate attempt at controlled calm, Lee said 'James, take me back home, please. Take me home, because this is no good. It's not going to work.' She spoke as firmly as she could but inside Lee felt forlorn and deadly, disconcertingly, sober. James leaned across her and whispered obscenely that it was her and not Cara he wanted to take to bed, but he left the car and went up the path to the house anyway. Lee wondered if she ought to scramble out and go, and if so, where, but he returned quickly, saying evasively, 'They'll probably be along later.'

'James, they won't. Paul doesn't want anything to do with me, he's made that perfectly clear.'

'He does, Lee – he thinks you're fantastic, he's always saying so.'

Lee felt miserable and intimidated. If it had been possible, even then, to take advantage of the drunk, dark, laughter-sodden night and to have believed that, she would have done so. She had tried, but her mind flinched into a wizened little kernel of realism and would not let her indulge in that belief.

'James, please can we call this off. It's just... ridiculous.'

James started the car.

'Ridiculous? What's ridiculous.'

'This is. Please don't fuck me about if you want Cara. It's absurd.'

James was adamant. It was her he wanted, he insisted, and the car drove on to his flat. Lee thought, this is not only absurd, it's also pretty close to humiliating. But there was the rest of the night to try to alter this mood. Maybe by morning it will be ok, she thought, maybe then we'll have some kind of real communication, when he's not so tensed up. The thought of the night ahead appeared to be on James's mind too. 'A whole night!' he kept exclaiming, and Lee heard in his enthusiasm no hint of menace, no intimation of violent interruption. She relaxed a little.

It wasn't good from the start. Lee felt exasperated by James's frantic energy, earlier exciting and now seeming uncontrolled and unconnected to herself. Maybe, she thought, when he's come and calmed down I can make things nicer and more affectionate. Actually what happened at that moment was a climax of a different sort: the repeated and violent ringing of the front door bell. James was off her like a fire cracker.

'Get your clothes on,' he hissed, piling his own back on with frenetic speed. Lee, slow and cross, climbed back into her things in silent exasperation. If that's Fionnula, she thought, I suppose there'll be a bloody awful row.

It was not Fionnula. The figure who stamped into the room, white-faced, blazing-eyed, with lips tightened in menace, was Cara.

It was Cara's silence that Lee found most scary. Her silence was a brittle force that seemed to seal every object in the room into a breathless vacuum and to erase every fragment of external noise, as though all sound and movement was cancelled by her will of frozen silence. Lee had never yet met a situation in which she found nothing to say and simply couldn't imagine the place of emotional intensity where her friend was now, as she stared silently at Lee with blazing eyes . At Cara's entrance, Lee had instinctively uttered her name, which now shrivelled in the vituperative echo of silence. She turned to James.

'What's going on, James?'

'Let's all have some coffee!'

'Don't be daft, James, who wants coffee?'

'I do – you do – Cara does. We'll all have coffee.' And laughing nervously, James escaped to the kitchen.

The two women were left looking at each other. Cara on entering the room had strode across to the mantlepiece, where she now stood leaning, regarding Lee steadily and unflinchingly. Lee could not return the gaze. The malevolence in those eyes was devastating, but even more of a deterrent to Lee was the hurtful absurdity of this situation. There must be something she could say to break the spell and turn this avenger back into a verbal human again. She searched for the sort of words that might do this – ironic, flippant, questioning, joking – some tone that would normalise and redeem the situation. But she could find no words, and without words she was without dignity. Cara held all the dignity in the power of her anger, and not for one second would she let it falter.

The moments passing now became elongated, like in a car crash. She had time to recall her earlier sense of Cara a powerful warrior queen – what was her name? Gráinne, or Granuaile, standing resolutely against her English enemies. She had time to reflect that James came from protestant stock, Ireland's invading rulers, and to remember the legend that the Earl of Howth had tried to stand against her and been cursed until he promised to leave a seat for her at his table forever. She had time to wonder what the fuck James was playing at, as banal comments on the progress of the coffee-making filtered through the door.

Abruptly Cara now spoke, calling into the kitchen a savagely-spoken humourless insult to James's coffee-making abilities. It was clear she was asserting a habitual authority. Lee looked around for her coat as James came in with two coffees, both spilled in their saucers.

'I don't want coffee, James. I'm going now.'

'I'll run you home.'

'Home?' Lee's indignation seemed suddenly offered an outlet. 'I'm not going home to stage a dramatic interruption!' She still couldn't look at Cara but managed an emphatic emphasis, which James completely ignored.

'Where are you going, then?'

So had King Richard been asked after his abdication, in Shakespeare's version of the monarch's humiliation. *Whither you will, so I were from your sights'* he had spat at his tormentors, and been imprisoned in the tower for his defiance. Strange the things that come to mind in extremis, thought Lee, and she answered fiercely. 'I'm just going. Leave me alone.' She pushed past him and headed down the stairs, pulled open the door and ran down the path to the street.

It was a cold night, but clear. Trees overhung the road, blowing noisily in the wind and obliterating any reassuring traffic sounds from the main road, and it was very dark indeed. Lee started to head in the direction of Melissa's flat. Melissa would surely be back from her babysitting by now, she thought. She hurried along, commentating ferociously to herself, mustering words to protect her fragile dignity: 'bloody idiot… ridiculous farce…' – comforting, cross, words, that would eventually contain this episode and force it to submit to mere absurdity. Behind her she heard a car and turned to see James driving up close to the kerb alongside her. He had the window down and was leaning across the passenger seat to call out to her. In the back seat, serene, smoking, unspeaking, sat Cara.

'Lee, don't be daft. Get in.'

Lee felt calmer and more in control now that she had left the flat, but not much. Her escape might have been meaningless but the chase gave some form and validity to it, and she felt very nearly jubilant. Cara's choice to join in the pursuit also made Lee feel a renewed triumph in resistance.

'No thanks. I'd rather walk.'

She maintained her pace and after a moment the car regained her.

'Lee!'

'You again James? You are having a lot of trouble with your women tonight.'

The trite grimness cheered her: she was regaining strength. She had a sense of the two figures in the car as tribal figures, one from each side of the bigotry divide yet connected despite the pull of their warring ancestors, and from this a consciousness of her own irrelevance in a conflict much deeper than this tawdry struggle.

'Please get in, Lee.'

'No thanks. I've no desire to prolong this ridiculous farce.

Now please sod off.'

She was aware the car had stopped now and was resting at the kerb behind her as she continued clattering down the road in breathless, childish, triumph. She reached the corner to the main road. Through the rustling of the trees, she could hear the faint sound of a car turning and retreating.

Lee strode on, unbothered by the potential hostility of the night streets. She felt she had arrived at a revelation. How could she have been so stupid as to think she could find a place in this conflicted community? She was living in Ulster, probably now the most hostilely-divided city in the world, and she came from the tribe that had made it so. She remembered the Orange March the previous year that Bruno wouldn't let her go to watch. 'You can't take the kids, it's not safe,' he had said, 'You can smell the hatred in the air – it's thick enough to slice. You'll never wash it out of your head. I know you Lee, you'll have nightmares.' Now she felt overwhelmed by sense of her own irredeemable Englishness, and Cara's essential need to regain her power over her own domain and heritage. Isn't it in chess, Lee wondered irrelevantly just before sobriety reclaimed her, when the queen comes back as a pawn, but the king is never allowed to return to the game at all.

Lee's initial elation had dispersed, leaving her uncertain what to do. She had vehemently denied any intention of returning home but she couldn't think of any alternative as Melissa's, on reflection, was impossible, as since Bruno and Elaine had returned together this would immediately mean awkwardness. And apart from that, Lee cringed at the thought of Melissa's inquisitiveness and avid interrogation which she felt would seduce her into analysing an episode she needed first to accept in its actuality. Ultimately I can lighten it, she thought – people use the means available to them to survive and belittling is one of them. I'll have to see it as funny. It was certainly absurd. I'll just have to digest it in mirth and self-mockery.

But first she had to swallow down the awfulness. Lies had

prevailed, lovelessness had predominated, and ultimately just silence and a nervous man jittering about with coffee cups and wondering how to get one woman out to make room for another. It was the stuff of farce. How funny, commented Lee to herself, acidly, and then she reflected that they, too, would have something to come to terms with. They'll use what they can too, she thought, same as me – humour from mockery and contempt. With me in the frame in their version. It's inevitable, it doesn't really matter. They'll be sealed together by now in the security of their union against me. I suppose every episode is educative if you survive it, even humiliation and rejection.

Lee realised she had anyway passed Melissa's flat by now, and was filled with a longing to go home. I can sleep on the mattress in the living-room, she thought, that won't bother them, and she hurried on through the black, patchily shining, streets to the flat.

She had overlooked the problem of getting in. The front was of course securely locked until the shop re-opened again, and though the gate to the back yard was open, the door at the top of the fire-escape stairs was also locked. Lee hadn't brought her yale key, and her repeated banging produced no response. She remembered the time the policeman had tried to kick it in, and lacking the constabulary-issue boots, looked around for a big stone or a block of wood that might make similar impact. But Bruno had been conscientious in clearing the back yard of anything that might be used to assault their windows, so she only had her high-heeled boots which made little impact. Ten minutes passed, and Lee, despite her frantic emotion, with only her lacy white cotton party dress below her duffle-coat, was feeling close to frozen. Thank christ I'm drunk, Lee thought through shuddering breaths, I'd freeze to death if I knew how cold I was.

She focused on contemplating her alternatives. They all seemed hopeless. I'm not going all the way back to Melissa's, she decided, and I can't go to Ian's after that fiasco the other night. Sam's nearest, but he's away. After that, Paul and Cara's. Impossible. But if Paul left the party when Cara did, he would be home by now. He could hardly refuse to give her refuge for the rest of the night. Perhaps this time they had got a baby-sitter, rather than leaving Samantha alone. Before she had fully clarified her rationale, Lee was walking down the familiar, dismal, terraced street.

It was so silent she felt furtive at first, and then defiant. Her footsteps were loudly audible and seemed to continue for an unusually long time before she reached the door of the familiar terraced house. There was a light behind the curtains in the upper front room, which Lee now knew was Paul and Cara's bedroom. Not that that necessarily gives any indication who is in there, Lee reminded herself, but something stubborn within her persisted in the belief that Paul there, and that he was alone, and that he was quietly waiting for her with a complete explanation of everything, which would take her tenderly back in time to those exultant days when love seemed to be all around them. Lee rang the bell.

It was one of those quasi-melodic two-tone bells that seem more suited to a flowery-gardened semi than a grimy terraced house in a vicious backstreet. Bing-bong. There was no answer. Lee rang again. Bing-bong-bing-bong. The mincing pretentious sound reverberated las if the street was holding its breath. Bing-bong-bing-bong-bing-bong. Lee was ringing repeatedly now, sobbing silently as she pressed again and again and again. The little plastic knob kept getting stuck from the force of her pressure and she had to pick it back with her nails, making the disjointed ringing sound even more derisive. Bing... Bing... bing.

Curtains twitched in the next door house. Lee left the step and began to walk slowly back down the street with tears streaming her face.

'God, how awful,' said Elaine sympathetically. It was next day.

Lee's tense and sleepless night was over, the children were up, dressed and breakfasted, playing quietly, and Lee had brought a tray with coffee and toast to the bedroom, where she, Bruno, and Elaine now sat together on the bed. Lee was regarding the familiar blankets with approval. She had eventually woken Breff by banging the door with a large stone for what seemed like half an hour, and Bruno, staggering sleepily in to comfort his crying, had at last heard her. Lee had gone at first automatically to the bedroom, where Elaine lay sleeping. She had knelt at the side of the bed and laid her head tiredly against it, breathing long sighs of relief. Bruno stood rather uncertainly beside her, stroking her head, until Lee whispered, 'I'm going to sleep downstairs. I'll tell you about it in the morning.'

'Are you sure that's alright?' Bruno asked quietly.

'Yes, fine.' Then, 'Kiss me, darling?' They embraced quietly. Lee whispered 'I love you Bruno,' and he said gently 'I love you too,' before Lee collected her dressing gown and quietly left.

The account had now reached Cara's arrival.

'Yes, it was awful. She was raging – too angry to speak.'

'What on earth was she raging about?'

'Well, me, I suppose. I think James had persuaded himself everything would work out fine, regardless of realities. Maybe she didn't even know I was there.' Lee did not remotely believe this but was still reluctant to face the full extent of planned ruthlessness with which her friend had confronted her. 'Anyway it was ludicrous after that. James seemed really scared of her and was farting about making coffee while Cara just stood there shooting dagger looks and not answering anything I said, and I was afraid I'd start laughing out of sheer nervous hysteria.'

'Didn't she say anything at all?' Elaine asked.

'No – oh, yes, she bit James's head off at one point, I think he'd dropped the sugar. She didn't say anything to me.'

'How pathetic.'

'Yeah… but it felt horrible. So since there was no further role for me in this scene, I pushed off. They got automated and gave chase for a while, but I just kept making snotty comments until James gave up.' Lee felt her laconic summary trivialised the episode satisfactorily, both conveying the facts and salving her dignity. 'I doubt if it was a serious effort, she added, 'it must have been a bit grotty for him too.'

'It sounds as though he came out of this pretty poorly' said Bruno, not without a sharp note of satisfaction.

'He was pathetic. I felt sorry for him actually. But I felt much more sorry for me, stomping home all wounded dignity at 3 o'clock in the bloody morning! And then I couldn't rouse you. I even went down to Paul's place to risk a scathing reception there, but I didn't get in.'

'Was he still out?'

'Either out or not answering. I'm glad, in retrospect. I don't think I could have coped with any more confrontations!'

This was true, but Lee still had no idea what had driven her towards Paul's house, or why she had responded to the irrevocable negative offered there with such helpless misery. Had she really believed that she could calmly petition for a floor to sleep on and then remain there passively, to leave in the morning without beseeching him for some explanation. His silence was enough answer now: rejection was utter and total, and Lee had reached the end of this broken road at last. She could think of Paul without turmoil and with a curious objectivity. I'll never understand I got so hung up about a bloke I never even particularly admired, she thought, and we only loved for such a very little while, I really don't see why such a horrible mess should have ensued, but it did. She thought, for some strange sad reason, of the youngster shot dead on the streets of his home town, and the woman who had hated his tribe so much she played *Are You Lonesome Tonight* on air and said it was for his mother. She had believed they were making a different community, spinning the lottery of life to fall always on love and never on hate. But their world had become just as punitive as the hating world. Should people stop seeking connections and exploring ways of loving for fear of punishment? She had wanted too much, and she had not got away with it. Nobody gets away with anything, Lee thought.

Rain trickled down the window, sparkling in the lamp-light. Lee was glad of it. It meant the icy days were over, if the rain could flow down the panes without freezing.

14

EARLY SUMMER

WITH THE BETTER weather coming, Lee was able to leave the push-chair in the yard, with the back gate bolted, so it was easier to come and go, and she spent much of most daytime outdoors with the children. The Botanic Gardens had been revamped for the Ulster Exhibition, a much-derided attempt to counteract the bad press that the violence in the city was attracting, and there were beds of roses now, just coming into bloom. They fascinated Finn. Watching him looking with intent curiosity at their pale golden petals tinged faintly with pink reminded Lee of a photograph taken by her grandfather on his Kodak folding camera when she was about her son's age. She too had been standing beside a rose bush and absorbed in some private communion with it, when her mother had suddenly stooped to put an arm around her. Lee remembered feeling uncomfortable and somewhat embarrassed by the unfamiliar embrace, and being relieved when the photograph had been taken and her mother released her and stood up again. She still had the faded monochrome picture but couldn't remember what colour that rose had been.

Lee waited, watching Finn's quiet gaze transfer to another bush, and then a smaller bush with just one bloom. He scurried back.

'Mummy, this flower is sad! It's got no friends!'

'Yes it has, darling,' she reassured him, 'you're its friend!'

He contemplated, then smiled up at her. 'Yes! And the sun, and the sky, and all the world can be its friend.'

I will never be like my mother, Lee vowed, once again, I

will make sure my children feel always surrounded by love.

But then, how could she? she thought as he danced away. Your children are not your children, they dwell in the house of tomorrow, which you cannot enter, not even in your dreams.

And now the sun was shining again, the conflict in the city was becoming increasingly visible. The suitcase and rucksack ready by their back window was becoming the epicentre of their life as shootings in the city escalated. Bruno, after leaving the house by the back door late one evening, had returned abruptly looking shaken. 'I'd just got out the gate when I heard a voice in the dark saying "Turn that fucking light off and get back in the fucking house."

'Who was it?' Lee wanted to know, but Bruno shook his head . 'Fuck knows. Better not to ask.'

They had a visit from two police who said they'd been checking gun licence owners, and found a document that showed that Bruno was in possession of guns. Initially baffled, Bruno then realised these must be the hand guns he'd borrowed for the play the previous year, which he had – he assured them – returned to the sports shop, as a quick visit would immediately verify. Unfortunately it wouldn't, as the sports shop had been bombed earlier in the year. Interrogation at the police station took most of a day, but Bruno was eventually released. 'I thought I was headed for H-Block' he claimed in his dramatic retellings, but he was lucky: in the end it became just another good anecdote.

But they all walked more warily, watched the shadows, and listened more intently to street noises at night. Lee was frequently startled by the furious rattling of the empty cigarette machines in Mr. Smith's shop doorway late at night. 'Are they still functioning?' she had whispered to Bruno when he reassured her that was the innocent cause of all the commotion. 'I doubt they were still functioning when England lost India,' Bruno replied, 'but you know how it is: Hope springs eternal in the Belfast drunk's breast.'

Hope, or at least resilience, seemed to thrive as days grew longer. Warmer days were bringing more litter and a stickier dust as people began to linger in the streets rather than hurrying back indoors. Botanic Gardens were becoming a regular trip for Lee whenever the essential shopping was done and, as Bruno and Elaine were both on revision time, they often came with her.

On one idyllic day in May several of their group had joined them on the lawn beside the rose beds, which were now thickly populated with pink and golden blooms and protected by low railings. It was a proper summer picnic: Lee had made a big pack of sandwiches, reckless of expense – the price of a loaf was up to nine pee now. That's nearly two shillings, in old money, she mused, lavishing on the marmite filling. She had mumbled this protest in the bread shop and the girl said blithely, 'It's going up to ten pee soon.' Whatever happened to the good old ha'penny? Lee wondered: everything seemed to go up in leaps now.

Melissa had arrived while she was diluting orange juice to the children. Lee was pleased to see her, happy that they seemed somehow to have recovered easy-going intimacy of their earlier friendship. She did not intend to discuss the stresses that had stretched their mutual tolerance: it was that awful winter that seemed to go on forever, Lee had decided – the cold and darkness got everywhere. And we weren't so used the the dramas and tensions of the troubles, too, it was all displaced into personal stuff.

So she waved at her across the picnic paraphernalia still in preparation and said 'Look, I got this fab teeshirt in Woolies today – what do you think? as she gestured her breasts for admiration.

'Your colours!' Melissa conceded, smiling: ' Pink and purple and turquoise stripes, very you! '

' I know! I thought it would go with my patchwork skirt!' Lee curtsied to show that item better.

'Well, that's got so many colours it would be hard to find a top that didn't pick out some them,' Melissa agreed genially, settling a bag of apples in the pushchair carrier and turning her attention to the tee-shirt. 'You'd better catch that loose thread, Lee, or it'll unravel first time you wash it.'

'Ah, right. I guess that's why it was in the marked-down section. Only thirty bob, so I thought I'd splash out on something new for the summer.'

'You are funny Lee, the way you sometimes talk in 'old money' like a Belfast housewife! – you're full of surprises.' Lee giggled, putting on her idea of a Belfast woman's voice to croon at Breff, as she settled him between their picnic packs, 'Ah, would you look at him now, the wee dote!'

'Budder wouldn' melt innis mouth!' agreed Melissa, also in cod Ulster, and the baby laughed with them, wide-eyed.

It was Lee's turn to look after Samantha, who was currently upstairs with Finn, watched by Bruno and Elaine. For a couple of weeks after the Brown Sugar episode, as Lee had now filed her silent row with Cara, Samantha didn't arrive at the shop, and Lee made no attempt to revive their arrangement. The following week Cara had brought her again, smilingly explaining that she'd had a cold so it seemed best to wait till it was over. Lee made no comment except to agree, and although her contact with Cara was now muted, it was a relief that Finn had his playmate back, that Paul could call at the house again without her caring, and that while she'd never solve the mysteries of that night, she was content to stop brooding on it.

With the picnic complete, Bruno and the three women set off to the gardens with the three children. Once they'd reached their chosen pitch, two or three hours passed peacefully as they camped on the grass with the odd beer passed round, although later that night the radio told them that less than two miles away a British soldier during the afternoon had shot and killed IRA member Billy Reid in an ambush in Academy Street. (The chords of the ballad written in his honour, Bruno later told Lee, were very simple: G, D, and A.)

Melissa reminded Lee she'd promised to teach her how to do the yoga 'salute to the sun' series of poses and today seemed definitely the day for it, but Lee pointed out that her voluminous cheesecloth smock would make success difficult especially in a public place, and Melissa lay down on the grass instead. Even Samantha, who could be difficult to entertain, in this placid atmosphere behaved delightfully, and a game of chase-you-round-the-roses seemed so happily in progress Lee had only to shade her eyes from the sun and watch without any intervention required. Elaine was lying full length along the grass conscientiously cross-referencing several source books for a lecture on the Pre-Raphaelites the while Breff clambered up her prone body, giggling as he rolled down again.

Lee lay back on the grass luxuriating, and for the first time noticed the significance of the changed skyline just beyond the museum. She sat up, shading her eyes.

'That's the Ulster Exhibition, isn't it – is it open yet?' she asked, though without any real curiosity since she had no expectation it would be any more interesting than the aggressively mono-cultural bravado of the permanent collection. It was Sam who answered.

'Yeah, there's all kinds of stuff under those domes – slot machines, kiosks, donuts, ice-pops…' he caught Lee's eye-roll and laughed – 'Yeah, the apex of our culture is all on display! There's an afternoon disco too.'

'Have you been?'

'Sure. Try any drink once.'

'Would you go again?'

'Nah, it's all kids skiving off their books. Proddy ones, of course. It's a bit far off the track for the others, if you know what I mean. A long run home!'

Lee digested the inference and felt the familiar quiver of anxiety, in spite of the sunshine. She realised she still had no clear idea why it had appeared, so she said, to Sam or anyone in the group, 'What's it celebrating, anyway? I mean, why now?'

Sam was happy to answer that. 'Fifty years of Northern Ireland. The Act was in 1920, but it took till next year to get it sorted: Southern Ireland and Northern Ireland – they were supposed to stay together, just differently governed. But they couldn't agree on that either.'

Lee reflected. 'So... since the Act that was supposed to settle everything, it's been fifty years of division and unrest and conflict.'

'Aye,' Sam agreed, 'That's the Irish way.'

Lee lay back again. She thought back to the night in the Jubilee, when she had wondered why the shadow of the past still fell so strongly over them all. Fifty years would be actually in the lifetime of a lot of those men – and certainly in living memory for all of their families.

'It's funny to think of Northern Ireland as a young state – in the sense of a new nation,' she said, and Bruno, who was on his back reading, said without looking up 'Well it isn't. It's vassal state of England now.

'Hey, don't forget I'm English,' Lee protested, though pleased he was joining in the conversation.

'You? you're stateless – you're a free spirit from the land of your own imagination.'

Lee laughed. 'I dwell in the house of tomorrow? she suggested.

'You dwell in cloud cuckoo land, now let me get on with me book.' But Bruno did bend over her to give her a kiss so she took the chance to read the title of his book.

'*Catch 22*! Hey, that's not revising!'

'Good book. You'd like this, you know, Lee,'

She raised her eyebrows dubiously. 'It's about war isn't it?'

'It's anti-war, and it's funny. You should read it.' She reached out towards his copy but he pulled it away. 'Wait till I finish, you'll scribble all over it. I know you.'

'Why would I do that?' Lee protested as he hid the book

under his back,

'I dunno, but you always do.' He scrambled to his feet and held it aloft, laughing as she jumped for it. They were all giggling now, and the revision session collapsed completely when a football catapulted abruptly in their midst. Everyone sat up and swivelled around to see who, what, and why, and suddenly they were all on their feet, and the ball was getting belted back and forth in a small but gathering crowd. There were no particular goalposts, not even virtual ones, evident in this game of run-pounce-and kick, with the main aim apparently to keep the ball off the rose beds, either for fear of a stem breaking (Lee's worry) or a thorn puncturing it (Bruno's concern). Lee had clipped Breff back into the pushchair in case someone tripped over him, and she was pleased to notice how all the adults slowed or stepped back when any of the children were near the ball, and would wait as long as it took until they had managed their own stumbling kicks.

Eventually energies ran out, and after cheerful farewells to those they knew and didn't know, they ambled back in sunshine. 'Whose ball was it?' Lee wanted to know, but no-one in the posse could remember if they even knew. Lee was fully satisfied with this sociable ignorance. I love these days, she thought with quiet exultance: this is how life should be.

The group gradually dispersed, Samantha was returned, and Lee and Bruno reached the shop. Lee paused outside, thinking of the stuffiness of the flat above. She looked at Bruno, also pausing as if reluctant, and indicated the now-exhausted baby asleep in the pushchair, 'We could leave him outside, just for a bit, rather than wake him by lugging this thing up the stairs. I'll take the bags off and put the hood up a bit to shade him, and we can keep an eye on him from the living-room.'

'You can't see the street directly from the living-room unless you're right by the window,' Bruno pointed out, 'You'll have to keep an eye from pretty close.'

'Oh I will,' Lee promised, and she did, checking he hadn't

woken every few minutes until quite soon a time came when there was nothing to check. The push-chair had disappeared.

Lee didn't scream because her throat, like the rest of her, had somehow both frozen and melted. Bruno, hurrying over in response to her incoherent gasps of anguish and grief, held her to calm her shaking. 'He may be in the shop – someone may have brought him in. Or if not, we'll go round to the cop-shop. They may know something – someone may have seen -'

Lee's primitive brain was already calling for the police, and she instantly started running for the door. 'You stay here, we can't both go –' she instructed with a coherence that surprised herself, and she hurtled down the stairs.

The push-chair was not in the shop, and Lee didn't pause as she dashed through the door into the main street and rounded the corner into Donegal Pass where the Police Station stood huddled behind its sandbag defences. Corrugated iron barriers and coils of barbed wire around the entrance made the place look like a set for a dystopian horror movie and an armed policeman stood by the doorway which was narrowed from its usual size by heavy metal sheets like those that entirely covered the windows.

Lee almost shoved the cop at the door, ignoring his gun and shouting 'My baby – someone's taken my baby.'

'Stop right there,' came the calm reply, and she had to, as the gun was now focused directly and firmly on her. 'Now, take a wee step back. There y'are! Now, what's the problem?'

Lee sobbed out, 'Someone's taken my baby.'

The policeman digested this repetition as though it was only now audible to him, and said, still slowly and calmly, 'Where from?'

'Right outside where we live. Just up there – Botanic Avenue – please let me in! I've got to talk to somebody.'

A voice from the shadows now chipped in 'she doesn't think you're somebody!'

'Ye're talkin' to somebody, ye're talking to me,' said the cop sternly, 'And you can't just barge in there till ye's told me exactly what ye're talkin' aboot.'

Lee felt like screaming and then tried hard to focus on what it was like to be a policeman in Belfast, never knowing what excuse someone was going to dream up to breach your fortified station. The attempt took about three seconds before she burst into sobs and the policemen decided it was safe to to help her out.

'When did yer baby go missing?'

'Ten minutes ago – no more, maybe less. Please help me!'

The second cop had emerged now, to help the first one look her up and down. They both did so, and then the one who had turned out to be somebody after all nodded to the other one. 'Take her inside, Tommo.'

Tommo beckoned Lee forward and ushered her through the narrow passage beyond the front line of sandbags. Just before the actual door, he paused to run his hands up and down Lee's body. 'Sorry,' he said, not looking at her, 'Protocol, have to check before youse go inside.' Like, where would I hide my suicide bombs under this, Lee had time to think, staring down at her rainbow coloured flimsy attire.

Satisfied, he conceded entry with a brief 'Follow me.' and they stepped into the reception area which, in contrast to the sun outside, seemed briefly to be in total darkness, and then as her eyes adjusted she saw her pushchair.

Breff had not even woken. Lee's streaming tears of relief impeded her full account to the duty policeman and it was hard not to grab her child from his comfort just to feel him in her arms but she managed it, partly because she was becoming aware they were not alone in the room. Two old ladies were now advancing on them, looking to Lee's still-frantic mind like mythic birds of prey – the evil child-snatching harpies from Hades. Like the chorus in a terrible Greek drama, they closed in on her now, chorusing as if they had rehearsed their accusatory chant, 'You left him an hour! You left him an hour!'

Lee howled her denial, and it was only much later it occurred to her that they had probably only just arrived and were still giving their spurious report to the police, and needed to agree on their story as an excuse for their kidnap. Lee sobbed her refutation with the two old ladies still jabbing at the air ahead of her, until the young cop on duty stepped in to suggest that the ladies should desist, and that Lee should depart. He held up his notebook and tore up his report to support his preferred outcome, and they all vacated the police station, blinking in the sunlight outside.

Lee set off towards home, still shaking, tears still streaked down her face, ignoring the scolding voices behind her chorusing their overlapping curses: 'Not fit to be a mother' – 'Should be ashamed of yourself, leaving a baby in the street like that' – 'Deserve everything you got!' As soon as she felt far enough away to be safe from them, she scooped her baby up to hold him tight, pushing the chair mainly by her tummy, and took him home.

It took Lee a while to calm down and completely reassure herself that Breff was safe back in her care now, and had never even roused to know the drama around him. She couldn't stop trembling all the rest of that day. 'How could they do that?' she repeatedly asked the air around her, 'how could they take him away like that – pretend he was abandoned – not even call in the shop to ask?'

'Perhaps they did,' Bruno said, 'Old Smith isn't the most communicative of blokes at the best of times. If he was taking delivery of twenty pee for a packet of fags, that would be his priority, even if the wain was screaming blue murder.'

Lee knew that was plausible, but even now her baby was safely home she shuddered at the idea he might have woken and cried. She suspected that Mr Smith, like the old ladies who'd sanctimoniously stolen her child, would stand in judgment of her parenting skills, satisfied that she had been shown up and called out. 'This place,' she stormed, 'These people…' – and as another disturbing aspect occurred to her, 'The police know us, now, Bruno, they know we've complained about our home being targeted, and now they know I'm not liked around here – but they do know we're not conspirators, just students?'

She started to remind him, but couldn't remember the name of the road in the news item, that it was only a week since a loyalist bomb thrown into a shop had started a fire that killed a woman living in the flat upstairs.

Bruno needed no such reminder.

'That was the other side of the river, love' he said soothingly, as though two miles distance and a river around eighty metres wide would somehow ensure their continued safety. Lee continued to look distressed so he answered her question.

'They know we're not Taigs, but they also know we won't be cheering the Orange brigade on the Twelfth, Lee, and that makes us kind of gypsies to some of the folks in this area.'

'It's a big gypsy convoy, then,' Lee responded, 'Loads of people round here are students.'

'And loads aren't. D'you think they feel comfortable with us lot milling about? It's going to get worse everywhere, Lee. I'm just thankful term's nearly over and keeping me fingers crossed that one of my applications gets accepted. Then we can get the fuck out of here.'

It was coming up to the marching season. The previous year Lee had watched, fascinated, on their small rented TV these parades for the Glorious Twelfth in July, imagining how vibrant and impressive the scene must be in colour and for real. Scores of men holding big flags and shared banners leading the massed marching musicians and hundreds of men, women, and children keeping step with them as they strode alongside. A host of girls in tartan skirts with accordions, boys in black with red caps and flutes, and then a phalanx of men in bowler hats with golden sashes around their sombre suits.

'Who are they?' Lee had asked, fascinated but quailing a

little at the ferocious determination in their expressions.

'Twats,' said Bruno, without even looking.

Now came the women, dressed with big hats and white gloves as if for a wedding, and then more banners, tall as their bearers, with images of curly-whigged, scarlet-coated, King Billy crossing the Boyne on a white horse rampant. Lee recognised the piped strains of 'The Sash Me Father Wore,' and hummed along

'- and it's on the twelfth I love to wear
the sash me father wore.'

She swayed Breff in time to the tune and Finn banged together the two plastic building beakers he held.

'Lee, for fucks sake,' Bruno said.

'What? I've heard you sing it, at parties.'

'Yeah, at parties. With our crowd, it's a joke about these cretins. When you're out and about you don't want the kids singing it like it was their bedtime nursery rhyme.'

'You want me to turn it off?'

'It's OK. You wanted to see it, and at least this way you'll know why I wouldn't let you go off yourself. You really wouldn't want to get caught up in that lot.'

The march seemed unending. More bands led by drummers, more men with sashes, another posse of wedding-guest women, more piped medleys and Lee realised there were scores of marching bands here, and hundreds of watchers lined up applauding them all.

'No police supervising,' Lee realised, 'Are they marching too?'

Bruno nodded. 'Mostly.'

'What would happen if they tried to go through a Catholic area?'

'Watch the news tonight and you'll see,' Bruno said calmly. 'Put it off now, love, will you – you've got the gist of it.'

Lee turned the knob and the image fizzled into a tiny white dot and faded. It was true she had seen enough, but she wondered if she would ever fully get the gist.

This year Lee had got a temp. job as as shorthand typist at the local mills as soon as the end of term released Bruno for daytime child-minding. She took the job without working out the rates of pay, hoping to be pleasantly surprised on the first Friday lunchtime trip to the agency, but actually the pay was remarkably poor. She felt indignation on behalf of the women of Belfast who habitually tried to support their families on such meagre wages, but on her own behalf she felt nothing but a sense of respite – despite the sharply critical comment on her attire that followed her out of the room. She replaced her beaded kaftan with less esoteric attire the following week, though with reluctance as it had been comfortable and deliciously cool.

The work was not arduous and, even better, it was constant. From the moment she uncovered her typewriter in the morning to the moment she reluctantly recovered it at five, there was a steady, liberating, stream of undemanding tasks. She had to take down, in shorthand, communications concerning materials: their dimensions, colours, attributes, and postulated arrival dates. These she then transcribed in an unvarying formula: even the address of the destination had a specific place on the letter-paper, indicated by an almost imperceptible dot. She had to type telex in upper-case on paper headed for that purpose, and complaints to the mill went on pink forms. Copies of all these missives were placed appropriately in their labelled locations. At the end of a satisfying day of simple tasks completed, the accumulated pile of correspondence, all filled with neat lines of words and figures, all duly signed in the correct place, was returned to Lee for folding in three places and placing in the envelopes which she had already addressed to correspond with the recipients. An airmail sticker was then attached if appropriate. Finally, all destinations were noted in a small blue book, kept for this purpose. Then the letters were removed from Lee's hands and knowledge and responsibility. She was free to descend, anonymously, the dark oak stairs, open the glass-fronted double doors, step out into the warmth of summer evening and walk slowly home, enjoying the anticipation of the next day's return.

Her role in the mill was, for Lee, the most rewarding experience she could ever remember undertaking. In place of the messy emotionalism of house and home, where nothing is ever finally settled, no issue closed forever, and no task really completed, it gave her a sense of immense tranquility to seal the manilla envelopes and dismiss them forever, without guilt. She sat serenely conscious of her enjoyment on the plastic office stool, sticky with heat, in the big old-fashioned room. Everyone was hot. The men who dictated the letters sweated and pulled at the inside of their shirt collars with moist tubby fingers as they contemplated the labelled scraps of stuff, lauding them in sporadic bursts of languid recommendation. Lee pulled her denim micro-skirt around warm thighs, shifting stickily and mentally measuring the samples, anticipating the most suitable size to select from her drawer of options.

Twice a day a ten minute break was allowed. In the first few days Lee had trecked through the vast halls of brown-paper-wrapped bales of fabric to the canteen for her cup of tea, but was quickly depressed by the instinctual sex-and-role segregation there. Instead she took to sitting in the Ladies' cloakroom with a plastic cup of coffee from the machine in the corridor. This was where the less-elevated female employees congregated, perching along the long bench below the pegs, staring incuriously at the mirrored faces replenishing lipstick or combing hair. They talked of their families – not, which perplexed Lee, of their husbands but of their 'mammies'. Most of their evenings appeared to include the relief of a trip 'home' to these mammies. For some, this happened when the husband returned home from having his evening meal at his own mammy's. Lee sat quietly digesting all these slivers of insight into this other universe, as some half-comprehending traveller might observe the marital rituals of a strange tribe.

One of the women was a dressmaker, not professionally but considered expert at the craft, and she used the Ladies as her fitting-room while the row below the pegs nodded approvingly.

'Lovely bit of crimpa-leen there.'

'Oh, it is – lovely.'

'Crimpa-leen always looks lovely.'

'And it does suit your size, Norma. It makes you look less big than what you are.'

'Do you think so?' This said with great contentment, as if at some subtle and loving observation. Perhaps it was.

'Oh, it does. It makes you look less big than what you are.'

'Do you think so?' Again the satisfied tone, plump hands smoothing plump thighs.

Lee watched, adoring and fascinated, as the endless low-decibel enthusiasm flowed across the washbasins. After a while she tried to break into this world where somehow, imperceptibly, these vague interchanges blended to enclose an intimacy that seemed so enviably undemanding. The inconsequential comments she cautiously added, haphazard as pollinating seeds, into the general converse, had been progressively reciprocated and Lee was emboldened to try out a pattern she had previously observed, by taking in a photograph of Finn and Breff to show at break-time.

The women in the Ladies cloakroom gathered around it and their mouths slackened into smiles from a habit of worried concern for the young of their species as they gazed at the snapshot smiling faces of the two little boys with their eyes screwed against the sun.

'They're not like you. Do they favour their father?'

Lee tried in her mind to relate the two worlds: this strange sanctuary where she now stood, and the other one.

'I suppose they do really.'

Fairly soon after that, regretfully, Lee left the office for the last time. She and Bruno were leaving Ireland. They had handed in their notice, packed up all their possessions into three trunks and a crate, roped up the cot and the pushchair, and they were quitting Belfast with its weekly rain of CS gas, its scrawled walls and houses, and the street where fire-engines daily whined and shrieked their way towards some burning debris of habitation. They had said goodbye to all their friends, and with every farewell Lee was assailed with unexpected nostalgia, like a moth in a cocoon struggling for flight yet fearful of it, or a soldier so long entombed in the trench that rescue becomes more frightening than remaining.

'What do you want to leave for?' asked Bruno's tutor, an irrepressible optimist – as he needed to be, being a Marxist in the Malone Road, '– it's got a fantastic war-time atmosphere, you won't find anything like this in England.' Shortly after they left, they read in the papers that a policy of internment without trial had been introduced in Northern Ireland. Over three hundred people considered republicans were arrested in pre-dawn raids by British security forces and held in Long Kesh prison. Twenty people died in the riots that followed. Bruno's tutor and other lecturers at the university were among the first internees, and Lee never knew whether the war-time atmosphere was something he continued to prize during his long stay in prison.

Now that they were going she could meet Paul on a near-normal level, but it still felt as though they were on different sides of an invisible crack that ran the length of the world. Their goodbyes had been muted yet enigmatic. 'You nearly upset my life completely, too' Paul said quietly after Lee had fumbled for some words to tell him something immense, yet perhaps untruthful, that she believed explained how he had become central in the implosion of her life's philosophy. He said it calmly, as one might muse over some half-remembered card game at which the stakes had been too high for the players. 'Things were quite rough for a while, for me.' He shook his head gently as if the sad slow movement would explain, but his eyes were secretive and his meaning was totally obscure to Lee. But it didn't matter, now. They were going, that was all.

15

ENGLAND

LEE WROTE to Melissa:
'I'm very much better now we're settled over here, thank
goodness. My doctor here thinks all my sickness was probably
tension, and Breffy's too! It just shows – I'm finding it so much
easier to cope. The last time I felt really ill was just after we got
here, when there was carnival bunting across the street and one
of the flags was a Union Jack. I literally retched, my stomach
felt like it had been punched, and then I realised the bloody
flag wasn't a symbol, it was just a decoration, because we were
in England, and they just saw it as decoration! Isn't Unionism
a terrible thing? They've completely mixed up religion and
politics so that it's inextricable, and the religious values have
simply evaporated. Do you remember Elaine's story about
when she first went to Ulster some man told her she'd have
to get a religion if she was living there and she'd better choose
Unionist. I thought it was so funny at the time, I wrote it in my
diary, that's how I remember. 'I'm not talking about politics,' he
said, 'I'm just telling you, get a religion and you'd better choose
Unionist.' Such an unbelievably vicious culture. Incidentally,
did you find out anymore about how Nathan got killed? It was
such a shock, to see it in the English papers.'

They had read about Nathan's death shortly after arriving.
The news item gave his name and age, and said he was in the car
of a visiting photo-journalist, alone, when it exploded and he was
killed outright. Bruno had in fact uncovered a more sinister and
sadder tale. Nathan had rashly agreed to take the journalist to a
pub in the Falls area to get his story, and he had waited outside.

He'd been grabbed, hooded, and shot in the back-alley where his fallen body was found some days later. The consensus among his friends was that Nathan had no paramilitary connections and was only trying to make a bit of money to get himself out of the city. Remembering his suicide bid, and all their efforts to encourage and rehabilitate him, Lee found herself more sad than shocked. *'What made fatuous sunbeams strive to break earth's sleep at all?'* was all she was able to say to Bruno, and he had understood the reference to Wilfred Owen's poem mourning a different death in another war, and hugged her for a while.

Lee never talked about such things to her neighbours or the mothers at the playgroup. Partly this was because she had been surprised to discover that 'over the water' there was very little understanding of, or will to understand, the true situation, and partly because she felt that by her escape she had cut herself off forever from the common currency of concern that only direct involvement allows. She felt guilty, in fact. So although she tried to keep the flow of her letters to Melissa sounding like the way they used to talk together, Lee sensed there was a subtle shift already and that her comments would sound increasingly hollow and unconnected as time went by.

As Ireland receded, inevitably, from her immediate awareness, Lee increasingly tried to use the distance to find the perspective that had been so elusive in close context.

It's twenty-five years, she thought, since the two tribal groups were told, like kids in a playground, to settle down and stop fighting, and it took from 1920 to 1921 to get both sides to agree even to the Act, and now the real backlash is beginning. And it was the British who started all the trouble from the start, when the Norman barons went over and seized the land, and then raiding Ireland just carried on, confiscating land from its Irish owners and handing it to English settlers – thousands of Cromwell's soldiers, all Protestant, granted plantation rights in land grabbed from Catholic Irish. One of the problems is, she thought sadly – and not for the first time – that Ulster's language sounds so like English. Half the time we think we understand each other when we really have no idea. What was it Melissa was always saying? 'The limit of my language is the limit of my world' – well that's true, but it's only half of it, language needs translation too. Or else we're all like the English in *A Passage to India*, putting our own construction on another culture, confusing courtesy with literal accuracy, and there's muddle and then tragedy. Only the Irish will always fight back.

She remembered a conversation she'd had with Bruno months ago, when the troubles were first starting.

'Cultural prejudice is the same as racism,' she had said, and he had nodded. 'Happens everywhere, Lee.'

'Racism,' she persisted, 'Talking about religion is just a cover up. I realised that when I read *A Passage to India* – '

'Great book,' Bruno said, patently aiming to distract her upcoming monologue. 'E M Forster was English, wasn't he?'

'Yes, but very critical of cultural divisions. His big thing was – '

'Only connect,' Bruno finished for her. 'I know.'

She focused on her letter and continued:

'Local shops here are really good – there's a sort of grocers that has all every spice you could want, in a rack. Schwartz, the make is called, and they do them all! There wasn't much spice in the shops in Belfast, was there? only the paprika!' We used it on everything, Lee remembered, even boiled eggs. She was running out of ways to describe her new life.

'I'm reading more, in the evenings – I've finished *Catch 22* – great book! I'll have to buy Bruno another copy, I scribbled loads of comments on his! And I've found a yoga class – it's in the hall next to the crèche, and Breff can come in with me! But it does seem terribly quiet here after Belfast, I still haven't got used to people not popping in all the time. It's not that they're unfriendly, they're just more formal and polite than I'd got used to. But it's unreal how safe it feels here. There's no vandalism, people put milk bottles on their steps at night – even early in the evening – and they're still there, not even smashed, for the milkman to collect up in the morning. They'll leave out their payment too, even – it's quite a usual occurrence! The street we live in is unbelievably neat, and the flower beds in the front gardens go right down to the pavement, sometimes even with a bit more on the pavement side of their hedge, and they're never vandalised! Remember those lovely roses they planted in the Botanic Gardens – the big creamy blooms with blush-pink tips? There's a bush of that sort next door, and I found out their name – they're called Peace roses. Funny really. Bombs and roses, that's how I'll remember Ireland. No-one here talks to people they don't know, though, and we haven't made any new friends yet. But did you know Elaine is over in England now too? She has a flat in London and she's been up to see us already. Bruno is staying down there this weekend and we're going to take it in turns to go down and have a weekend in London!'

Actually it didn't work out like that, because when Bruno returned it was to tell her that, now she and the children had settled in so nicely, he would be leaving her and going to live with Elaine. He had it all arranged – they seemed in fact to have arranged it between them some time ago, Elaine taking care to check that nothing that might cause Lee concern had been overlooked by Bruno in his logical, good-natured, settlement. He seemed now to be surprised and baffled by Lee's total stupefaction.

'Why didn't you tell me the truth about how it really was?' she kept reproaching him. Finally goaded from his calm attempts to discuss and reassure her on the practical side, he said 'You think "telling the truth" is pouring out a torrent of words and expecting the other person to understand what you mean, and what you want, and what you don't want. I couldn't give you a running commentary back then because I didn't know, half the time, how things would work out.'

'Talking would have helped both of us,' said Lee miserably,

'because then I wouldn't feel so dumped – even if you didn't want to discuss it, you could have warned me you loved her and that you might want to leave me.'

Bruno stared at her her a moment as though he found her words, which she believed to be so clear and reasonable, utterly unfathomable. Finally he said quietly 'I thought you knew.'

'How could I know if you didn't tell me?' Lee sounded plaintive and exasperated. He stared back and didn't seem to know the answer, or at least any answer she was capable of comprehending.

The night before he left she tried one more time. He had been for so long her best friend, her protector, interpreter, comforter, buddy, supporter and lover, but now in England perhaps most of these roles were redundant.

'Could you just tell me, in spite of everything, that you're glad you married me?' she pleaded, and Bruno sleepily murmured only 'Leave it, Lee.'

'That you don't regret it?' she persisted, 'Won't you at least say that?'

Bruno stirred almost as though he wanted to comfort her, but he said 'Lee that would be meaningless – I don't know what else might have happened.'

And only then in the emptied, pitiless, blankness of the moment, did she realise that they had parted long ago.

Why did it take me so long to grow up, thought Lee, feeling in a way almost impassive, as though the question were merely some metaphysical abstract – which perhaps, by now, it was. There was never any shred of a question in her mind that she might petition her mother for help, her memory was still raw with undigested recollections of their rows. 'You don't know how to live', her mother had shouted at her in exasperation more than once. Lee recalled mainly storms of tears in her bedroom after such confrontations, yet the time her mother had told her in mingled fury and reproach 'You are my only failure', Lee remembered she had found her voice briefly. 'I'm only sixteen,' she had said, 'You can't call me a failure yet.'

But in her mother's eyes, she was. She had dropped back in class grades, probably because of spending the evenings racing around on the back of a motorbike, and she wouldn't commit to become a secretary which according to her mother was the only option left to gain a husband of any quality. Lee had spent her entire childhood and early teens trying to make her mother love her, buying her presents with her pocket money and later with her Saturday earnings to atone for whatever the last row had been about – all coldly received with the mantra 'Sorry isn't good enough,' – and then she had discovered boys. Here was an easy way to feel loved. Her mother had scorned her abilities in everything she'd attempted, cancelled her place in the dance group because she was clumsy, abandoned her piano lesson because she was tone-deaf, stopped her cycling as she had no road sense, banned tennis because she kept apologising when she missed the ball, and any high-graded school work merely raised recollections of her mother's own achievements – which were, of course, better. There was only one exception: boys. Her mother never discussed sex, so once Lee discovered boys she found for the first time an activity where she could succeed and thrive. All this Lee now realised, belatedly and with gratitude for her mother's prudery. I was still a child long after I was married, she thought. I had two children, and no idea. Even in Belfast. Perhaps it took Belfast for me to grow up.

Lee went over to the photo albums, kept always accessible on the lower shelves. She turned the stiff transparent pages, flickering through the collage – wedding, travelling, first baby, until she came to the snaps of Belfast. They were instamatic images, mostly with flash, and the bleached laughing faces of that last year of her marriage seemed inscrutable now to Lee. Was I glad or sorry to go? she thought. We had some great friends, brave people who gave up their liberty for their beliefs, loving people who trusted our hippy code – crazy, colourful, people – but it all got so terribly confused. Lee watched the incoherent little images of her friends laughing and hugging each other with faces turned to the immortalising camera, remembering the last year of her marriage as if it were a long slow car-crash, from which thankfully she had been flung clear.

Bruno promised to help with her rent as he and Elaine both had jobs now, so without the stress of job-hunting or finding child-care, the days were in some ways not so different, although more repetitive. She heard on the radio that the civilian death toll in the Northern Irish Troubles had reached 100 after three years of violence, with the death of a little girl, Annette McGavigan, fatally wounded during crossfire between the soldiers and the IRA, and she was glad every day to have escaped with her boys to a place of safety. She missed nothing about her life there, not the parties or the liaisons or even the friendships. She continued to make toys and paint posters for Finn and Breff, trying to vary the focus each day apart from *Childrens Hour* on her rented TV, when they would sing along to the Trumpton fire-engine team: 'Hugh, Pugh, Barney Mcgew, Cuthbert, Dibble and Grub'. Lee worried that her boys' life was now so unpeopled, compared to the flat in Belfast, and made extra time to read to them each evening. At least, she thought, they had that wonderful start of being surrounded by an extended family of people who loved them – the closest I could get to a commune to nurture them. It was a relief that they still played together well, Finn telling stories to his brother while he manipulated dinky cars and farm animals around invented landscapes. Lee would sit sometimes watching them intent together. 'Then he went away' Finn said, moving a plastic cereal-packet figure along the floor, and Breff reached out his hand with an intrigued, interrogative, noise that his brother answered in the same engrossed narrative voice, perhaps interpreting it as a question, because he answered, 'No, he never came back.'

To eke out the quiet days Lee took the children often to

the park, where the gaunt trees were bare in the approaching bitterness of another winter. She knew that this unfamiliar landscape would soon merge with things known and things remembered. A walk in the park, talking to people I've not even yet met, thought Lee – it will all become as ordinary as instant coffee. I won't even notice the strangeness of the wavering outline of those trees, the endless gusting wind in this flat land will become normal, there will be reassuring voices in my life that now I don't even know. It was still impossible, even now, not to think of Elaine as a friend. She had been too long in the habit of loving her, and now she missed her acutely, with a sense of intense loss quite separately painful from the main sensation, of being Bruno-less. Sometimes she wondered if this was not missing, simply an expectation that his absence ought to feel like suffering.

Bruno hadn't yet visited but Lee found she was feeling increasingly positive in this strange new world where the police didn't wear guns. The women she met at the school gates were curious about Ireland, but they had no clear idea which were the six counties or whether she had lived in Dublin or Belfast. They would say, 'You must have been terrified of the IRA!', and after the bomb explosion at the top of the Post Office Tower in London in October that year, Lee stopped talking about any of it at all. She knew it would make no sense to them to say, actually the IRA were no problem for us, it was the Protestant extremists we had to be wary of. And anyway, what did she really know: she had been mistaken about so much, and everyone makes their own fear their reality.

But it would soon be over, they were saying now – there was going to be an agreement. Not a temporary stop, but a proper settlement, for all time. Too late to save her life with Bruno, but Lee realised now that would have gone anyway. Perhaps she was drained out, exhausted by the effort of continual anxiety, but now the sense of precariousness, that wary balance of uncertainty and hope had finally toppled, she found there was nothing further to dread. Every failure is a failure of love, Lee had argued, and she had always feared failure, yet now that failure had completely and irrevocably occurred, there was no more reason to fear.

The thought of returning to her childhood family home never crossed Lee's mind . She realised now, with a sense of calm purpose, that while she had been feeling increasingly guilty and inadequate within her marriage, the ending of it left her space to grow. And there was a reason to get up in the morning: two little boys, uncomprehending and innocent, who needed her reassurance and her love. Lee began to feel, as she focussed on these basic tasks, that this was her way back to self-belief. No longer could she take time out apathetically from the basic tasks of caring, comforting herself that these were being 'shared', now she could sit tiredly yet with a sense within that might yet grow into self-satisfaction: I bathed them, I read to them, we sang together – I tucked them up, and next I will try to fix that trike. In such tasks lay survival and might well become a way to contentment.

And there was another task Lee did not want to postpone. She knew she had somehow to consolidate the learnings of that last year. If all this suffering goes to waste, Lee argued to herself, then suffering is just a terrible thing with no purpose. But if I can make sense of that year in a way that contributes, in however tiny a way, to other peoples' understanding, of what was going on then that's a possibility of hope – not just for me, for everyone. It will mean that suffering can lead to learning, and learning can lead to hope.

What Lee had decided to do was to write a book. In the evenings, after she had settled the children and tidied up, she took out her desk-top typewriter, paper, and notes, and settled to the task of shaping an artefact from the confused rubble of her recollections. It was important to Lee to be precise. She had begun with a foreword:

The following account of events is based as closely as I can remember on real places and real people. However since reality is subjective, any resemblance to places or persons living or dead is unlikely. She struck a line through *'unlikely'* and changed it to *'merely coincidental.'* That was how you were supposed to do a disclaimer, wasn't it?

After this, however, she was stuck. She put the Peter Sarstedt LP they had played so often in the Belfast flat onto the record player, and let the familiar, evocative, words spill into her quiet new life.

'There is a torch-like face I will remember, that even I couldn't pass off as a joke...'

She pulled out her snapshots again, and looked at the flash-bleached laughing faces of last year, frozen forever in the mirth of that moment.

Lee tried again. Begin from right now, start with the passion that bombed my naive idea of free love, she thought, and she put a fresh sheet of paper in the typewriter.

'Brittle leaves gust past the window and the trees outside are bare in the empty dead of winter just before Christmas. Paul, I can't believe that you won't come come walking through the fallen leaves one day to explain everything...'

No, that was certainly not right. It spoke no kind of truth at all.

Lee put in another sheet of paper and clicked the return bar to roll it round for a new start. She tried to remember this night, one year ago. Was it really only a year? Hard to believe, but it was. A boy who's name she could not remember if she had ever known had whispered fiercely into her ear *'What's another slice off the loaf to you?'* and Lee had not known how to answer. Now, a year later, she had learned something very painfully, and she needed to find out what that was.

She would start with that night.

END

Crysse Morrison

My writing career is a patchwork portfolio. My two previous novels, *Frozen Summer* and *Sleeping in Sand*, were published by Hodder & Stoughton, and my short stories have been published in magazines and anthologies (including Virago) and broadcast on BBC Radio 4. I've written training books and computer programs aimed at teens, and articles on a whole raft of topics including creative writing, travel and photography (interviewing Linda McCartney was one highlight). More recently I wrote a non-fiction history of my present hometown, *Frome Unzipped - from Prehistory to Post-Punk*, which was commissioned by Hobnob Press.

Drama is a major interest: my plays have been professionally performed in Bristol and elsewhere, and I'm the south-west England reviewer for *Plays International*. I also write for a children's theatre company, and for a Pub Theatre company which performs in various upstairs rooms and once in a graveyard. While 'writer in residence' for Frome's Merlin Theatre, where I'm an associate artist, I started the Poetry Cafe in Frome, and have won several slams and performed my poems in a range of places including the top of the fourth plinth in Trafalgar Square! My collection *Crumbs from a Spinning World* is published by Burning Eye Books. There's more detail about everything on my website: www. https://www.crysse.com/

I now report weekly in my blog (https://crysse.blogspot.com/) on cultural events in and around Frome, but previously I led writing courses across the world from Thailand to Chile including several Greek islands as well as Tuscany, Spain, France, California – and Longleat Center Parcs. My proudest personal achievement was running a marathon in 4¼ hours, and my luckiest undeserved outcome is two splendid sons who both work in creative industries in the south-west.

This book has been somewhere in my head since I left Belfast in 1971 – the experience has never gone away.

Hobnob Press has been publishing books local to south-west England and by local authors since 1983. Full details at www. hobnobpress.co.uk.

9 781906 978853